TOM SWIFT
AND THE CITY OF GOLD

"Don't cut the cable—we'll blow up! Tom warned

TOM SWIFT
AND THE CITY OF GOLD

By
Victor Appleton II

original title: Tom Swift and His Spectromarine Selector

illustrated by Graham Kaye

TEMPO
BOOKS

GROSSET & DUNLAP, INC.
A National General Company
Publishers
New York

CONTENTS

CHAPTER I

MYSTERY CRASH

TWO giant cargo jets stood poised for take-off from the Swift Enterprises airfield. Eighteen-year-old Tom Swift Jr. paused at the top of the ramp to wave to his family and friends before stepping into the hatch of the leading plane.

"Good luck, son!" his father called out.

"Bring us back a gold statue from that underwater city!" cried Tom's pretty, blond sister, Sandra.

Her dark-haired friend, Phyllis Newton, blew a parting kiss to the young inventor.

"I'll see what I can find!" Tom grinned and waved. "Don't worry, Mom!"

The group had gathered to watch Tom's departure on a secret expedition to the South Atlantic. Employees of the Swifts' experimental station raised an affectionate parting cheer.

"I do hope this project of Tom's won't be too dangerous," Mrs. Swift murmured.

1

Mr. Swift, a tall, keen-eyed man, and one of the world's most distinguished scientists, put an arm around his wife. "Now, Mary! You know Tom has everything planned to the last detail."

Months before, in his diving seacopter, Tom had discovered a sunken city, apparently built of gold. It lay among a chain of undersea mountains known as the Atlantic Ridge. The young scientist-inventor was now returning to explore the ruins further with a new invention which he had recently perfected. Submarines to be used in the project were stored aboard the two cargo jets.

Tom stepped through the hatch and hurried to the flight compartment. Bud Barclay, his teen-aged chum and copilot, was at the controls. Lieutenant Cromwell, a Navy officer who was going along as an observer, occupied a bucket seat in one corner of the cabin.

"All checked out, Bud?" Tom inquired.

"Aye-aye, skipper. Ready for take-off!" The co-pilot added jokingly, "But how about a few more minutes to say good-by to Sandy?"

Tom winked at the lieutenant. "You had your chance, fly boy, while I was supervising the loading. Save the rest till we get back."

Bud pretended to groan. "Okay, Captain Bligh!" Then he broke into an excited grin. "No kidding, we'll really have something to talk about if those ruins turn out to be the famous lost city of Atlantis!"

"You said it, pal!" Tom's own heart was beating faster as he eased into the pilot's seat and slipped on his headphone.

"The tower says there's clear weather over the Atlantic," Lieutenant Cromwell remarked.

Tom nodded. "Should be a good flight!"

The boarding ramp was wheeled away and the powerful jet engines blasted into life. Last-minute instructions from the tower crackled over the radio. Tom and Bud gave a final wave through the cabin window and the huge ship went racing off down the runway.

In seconds they were air-borne. The vast Enterprises experimental station, four miles square and surrounded by a high concrete wall, lay spread out below with its white airstrips and gleaming modern laboratories and workshops. It was here that Tom and his father developed their astounding inventions.

"Here comes Slim!" Bud said as they circled for altitude.

The second cargo jet, under the command of Slim Davis, a Swift test pilot, was just taking off. It climbed steeply to join them.

"All set on course and procedure, Slim?" Tom asked over the radio.

"Roger! Lead the way, skipper!"

Leveling off, Tom sent his plane spearing seaward. Slim followed and swung into position abreast. Soon the two jets had left the coast behind and were soaring out over the Atlantic toward the southeast.

"Boy, what a picnic!" Bud exclaimed. "I've been looking forward a long time to exploring that city of gold!"

"Same here!" Tom's eyes flashed with anticipation. What was the secret of the strange civilization lost beneath the waves? he wondered.

"I understand this sunken city is somewhere near the Cape Verde Islands," put in Lieutenant Cromwell.

"That's right," Tom affirmed. "It lies north of the Cape Verdes along the Atlantic Ridge. Didn't Admiral Hopkins brief you?"

The Navy man shrugged. "Not too thoroughly. My job is simply to report your findings. He said the whole project was top secret."

"Naturally," Bud snorted. "Can you imagine what would happen if word leaked out about all that gold lying around unclaimed?"

Cromwell chuckled. "A submarine gold rush probably."

"Worse than that," Tom said gravely. "It could lead to real international trouble."

"I see what you mean." Cromwell's voice grew tense as he went on, "But what a setup! If that undersea layout is really built of solid gold, it must be worth more than Fort Knox!"

Surprised by the officer's greedy tone, Tom retorted, "We're not going just as gold prospectors.

This is a scientific expedition. That lost city may hold the answers to a whole flock of historical and geological problems!"

"Sure, sure, I understand that," Lieutenant Cromwell said hastily. "What's your plan of operation?"

Tom explained that he would create a giant air bubble around the site by means of his force-ray repelatron. He had used the same method in tapping a fabulous undersea bed of helium gas. This tremendous bubble of air, with its ceiling and walls of plastic, had become known as Tom Swift's deep-sea hydrodome.

"The hydrodome will provide a safe working space underwater," Tom continued. "Then I'll use my new de-organic-izer to—"

"Dee-or-what-izer?"

All heads turned at the gravelly voice speaking in a Western drawl. A bald-headed, bowlegged man came stumping into the compartment in high-heeled cowboy boots. He was Chow Winkler, former chuck-wagon cook from Texas and now chef on Swift expeditions.

"*What*-izer?" Bud hooted. "You mean what a shirt!" He added in shocked tones, "It *is* a shirt, isn't it? Or are you disguised as a walking neon sign?"

The stout Texan beamed proudly as he fingered the latest gaudy addition to his cowboy wardrobe. "Real stunner, ain't it, boys?"

6

"We're stunned, all right!" Tom chuckled as he removed his headset and flipped a switch to put the ship on autopilot. "Chow, if you weren't so valuable in the galley, we could put you up as a warning beacon at Enterprises!"

"Warning beacon my eye!" Bud needled. "We could sell that shirt to the Defense Department as a secret knockout device for enemy aircraft!"

Chow snorted disdainfully. "Reckon you're jest jealous o' this lil ole number, Buddy boy. But looky here, boss," the cook went on, turning to Tom, "what's this new invention o' yours I jest heard you talkin' about?"

"I call it a spectromarine selector. It's a de-organic-izer."

Chow shook his head in bewilderment. "Sure *sounds* grand. But I got an easier name for that steel cookshack on caterpillar treads I saw gettin' loaded into Slim's plane. I'm callin' it jest plain 'organ.'"

"Me, too," Bud agreed.

"You win," Tom said with a smile. "That is, outside of scientific circles. Anyhow, I aim to use the spectromarine selector for cleaning all the barnacles and slime off those undersea ruins so we can examine what's underneath."

"How's it work, boss?"

The young inventor became serious. "Well, Chow, that slimy coating on the ruins will still contain a lot of moisture, even after we create our air space. So my invention will first heat the stuff with infrared rays in order to boil off the moisture in the form of steam."

"Steam? Won't that be risky?" Bud objected with a frown. "Suppose you crack some of the pillars? You might bring a whole temple crashing down on our heads!"

"Yeah, like Samson did in the Good Book," Chow added worriedly.

"No danger of that." Tom took a piece of chart paper and made a quick sketch of his invention. "You see, there's a powerful vacuum pump at the rear of the housing, operating through a long hose with an intake at the front."

"What's that for?" Bud asked.

"I call it a localator vacuum producer. Maybe you remember from high school physics—"

"I probably don't, pal!"

"Well, anyhow," Tom went on, "under low air pressure, water boils at a low temperature. So the moisture will turn into steam without getting too hot. The same idea is used in producing evaporated milk."

"Oh, sure, I catch on now," Bud said.

"We can run the steam through a heat exchanger," Tom added, "in order to get back most of the energy we put into the job."

Bud grinned approvingly. "Pretty neat."

"How many o' these steam locomotive tank critters you got?" Chow asked.

"Just the one you saw," Tom replied. "They're expensive to build. But if my invention works, I'll have them made in small sizes for commercial use. They'd be great for cleaning and sterilizing food, soil, buildings and monuments, or what-have-you. And think how handy they'd be for cleaning up after floods!"

Lieutenant Cromwell asked with sharp-eyed interest, "Is that all there is to your invention?"

Tom shook his head. "No, there's also something called a semoreco unit, S-Co for short. This S-Co, by the way, is one reason I call the whole organ unit a spectromarine selector. It—"

"Good grief! *Look!*" With a yell of alarm, Bud pointed out the cabin window. "Slim's plane—"

The other cargo jet, flying a hundred yards to starboard, had begun weaving crazily off course! Slim's voice screeched over the radio speaker:

"Mayday! The ship's out of control, skipper!"

Tom snatched up the microphone, his eyes glued to the terrifying scene. "What's wrong, Slim?"

"Don't know! The controls won't answer!"

"What about your lifter jets?"

"No action! The lifter engine must've conked out, too!"

The huge plane was turning and twisting, losing altitude rapidly. Tom switched back to manual control, yelled a warning to Chow, and put his own ship into a steep dive.

"Great thunderin' bison!" The old cowpoke turned pale and grabbed wildly for support to keep from sprawling on the deck.

A deafening whine vibrated through the cabin as both jets plunged toward the ocean! Tom pulled out and leveled off with his lifter jets clear of the water. But the other ship struck with a shattering force amid geysers of spray!

"They're still afloat!" Bud cried.

Apparently Slim had regained enough control to ditch the craft. One wing was sticking up out of the water. Fortunately, the plane had tilted with its hatch topside.

"Abandon ship! Get out fast!" Tom urged over the radio. "We'll drop a ladder!"

As he snapped out orders over the intercom, Bud hurried aft to supervise the rescue operation. Slim's crew was already climbing frantically out of the doomed ship's hatch.

Tom locked the controls to keep the huge jet hovering in a steady position. Then he too dashed aft, followed by Chow and Lieutenant Cromwell.

"I sure hope we can save those poor hombres!" Chow gulped as he hurried along at Tom's heels toward the cargo compartment.

The rescue ladder was already being lowered. One by one, the stranded crewmen climbed to safety, swaying back and forth as they mounted the rungs. Tom and Bud helped them aboard.

Slim came last. He was halfway up the ladder

when the crashed plane finally nosed under and sank beneath the waves.

"Th-thanks, skipper!" Slim was drenched and

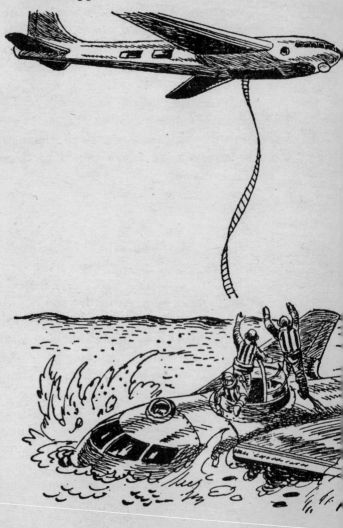

shuddering as Tom pulled him in through the hatch. "Believe me, I did everything I could to save the ship!"

"You saved your crew, Slim, and that's what matters!" Tom slapped him on the back. "Now you fellows get into some dry clothes. Chow, make 'em steaming coffee!"

"Sure thing, boss!"

Only the tight-lipped set of his jaw betrayed Tom's crushed hopes as he headed back to the flight compartment. Loss of the plane was bad enough. But with it, his prized spectromarine

The rescue ladder was already being lowered

selector had gone too, wrecking his carefully laid plans for exploring the city of gold!

Bud accompanied his pal in glum silence, but Lieutenant Cromwell remained aft. As they took their places at the controls, the radio suddenly crackled.

"Enterprises to Tom Swift! Can you read me?"

The young inventor flicked on his microphone. "Tom here! Come in, please!"

Harlan Ames, security chief of Swift Enterprises, was calling from Shopton. His voice sounded strained and urgent.

"Turn back, Tom! I'm afraid that you may have a saboteur aboard!"

CHAPTER II

THE IMPOSTOR

A SABOTEUR aboard! Tom and Bud exchanged looks of alarm as Ames cautioned, "Don't take any chances, skipper!"

"It's already too late," Tom reported grimly. "Our second ship just crashed and went down with my invention. But who's the person you're talking about, Harlan?"

Silence followed Tom's question. The young inventor hastily adjusted the radio tuning.

"Ames! . . . Ames! Can you read me?"

No reply. Apparently some freakish atmospheric condition had interrupted the broadcast.

"We'd better get back to Shopton pronto!" Tom decided. He gunned the lifter jets for quick altitude. Then, switching to the main engines, he banked the mammoth cargo plane in a smooth turn and set the automatic navigator on the homing beam for Enterprises.

"Who do you suppose Ames was talking about, skipper?" Bud asked tensely as they streaked toward the North American coast.

Tom shrugged, frowning. "I can't figure this out at all. Lieutenant Cromwell was cleared by Naval Intelligence, and every Enterprises air crewman has been double-checked by our own security department."

"What about a stowaway?" Bud suggested.

"We'll learn the answer when we land."

Both boys were grave as they mulled over this threat to Tom Swift's latest scientific undertaking. Ever since his first big invention, the atomic-powered Flying Lab, the young inventor had had to cope with enemies and spies bent on stealing his valuable plans for protecting American security.

As the cargo jet zoomed through the sky at supersonic speed, Bud asked if they should alert the crewmen over the intercom. Tom, however, decided against this.

"It'll be easier to trap our man if he doesn't realize we've been alerted," the young inventor pointed out.

Lieutenant Cromwell returned to the flight compartment as they came in sight of land.

"Tough break losing that other plane," the officer sympathized. "I suppose with your invention gone, the whole expedition is off?"

"For the time being," Tom said laconically.

In a few minutes the cargo plane streaked over Shopton and landed on the Enterprises airfield. A jeep came speeding out from the hangar apron. Harlan Ames was at the wheel. Mr. Swift was seated beside him.

Bud shot a questioning glance at Tom as they secured the controls. "Any *special* orders for the crew, skipper?" he asked guardedly.

Tom shook his head. "It's Ames's show," he murmured. "We'll see what happens." Switching on the intercom, Tom gave orders to disembark.

The crew filed out of the hatch, followed by Tom, Bud, and Lieutenant Cromwell. Ames and Mr. Swift stood by, grim-faced. As Cromwell stepped off the ramp, Ames confronted him.

"Don't move, Judson!" the security chief snapped. "You're under arrest!"

"Under arrest?" The accused Navy officer went sickly white, then spluttered, "You're crazy!"

"Get your hands up while I search you," Ames ordered.

He frisked the prisoner and found a small automatic neatly concealed in a shoulder holster. Tom and Bud were stunned by the sudden arrest.

"The real Lieutenant Cromwell was waylaid and robbed just outside of Washington, D. C.," Mr. Swift explained to the two boys. "Unfortunately, Ames didn't get word until after you had taken off."

Tom turned to the security chief and gestured

toward the prisoner. "Who is this man, Harlan, and what's his full name?"

"From the victim's description, the FBI was able to identify him as an ex-convict named Joe Judson," Ames replied. "He has already served time for embezzlement and he carried out the assault on Cromwell with a pal called Longneck Ebber. That's all we know so far."

"You're nuts!" the prisoner stormed. "I'll sue Swift Enterprises for false arrest!"

"I doubt it," Ames growled.

"What about his partner?" Bud spoke up.

"Ebber is still at large," Ames replied. "But he may not be for long after we jail his pal here."

"You've got me all wrong!" the prisoner insisted. "I'm Lieutenant Cromwell and these charges are false!"

"And I suppose that gun you were carrying was just for shooting fish," Ames retorted sarcastically.

"An officer has the right to carry arms."

"If that's a service automatic, I'll eat your gold braid!" Ames produced a pair of handcuffs and deftly manacled the prisoner. "All right, Judson, get into the jeep."

The prisoner sat in back, between Tom and Bud. Ames took the wheel again, with Mr. Swift beside him, and drove quickly to the Enterprises security building. Here the prisoner was fingerprinted.

Ames compared the newly inked prints with a

set forwarded from the FBI in Washington over the Swifts' private video network. "He's Judson, all right. These prints prove it."

Judson squirmed, red-faced. "Okay, so I'm Joe Judson. What about it?"

"You had free run of both planes before take-off," Tom said in an angry voice. "Why did you sabotage the ship carrying my invention?"

"Who says I did?" the prisoner snarled defiantly.

Ames snapped, "You'd be facing a murder charge if Slim Davis and his crew had gone down!"

"Well, they didn't and you've got a fat chance now of proving what caused the crash," Judson sneered.

Mr. Swift asked several probing questions, but the ex-convict replied stubbornly, "I've said all I'm going to say," and lapsed into sullen silence.

Mr. Swift turned to Ames. "We'd better let the authorities deal with him."

Ames nodded. "He'll talk eventually."

He picked up the phone and dialed head-quarters. Within minutes, a police car arrived at the plant and Judson was bundled off to jail. Tom then held a quick conference with his father and Ames to discuss the situation.

"If Judson was working for foreign agents," Mr. Swift said, "we may be in for serious trouble."

The distinguished scientist's face was grave as he outlined the possible dangers. "Once another nation learns about the city of gold, they're almost certain to send out undersea explorers of their own. They might even establish a claim before we can launch a fresh expedition."

Tom nodded. "That's what I'm afraid of. Our own government was depending on us before they made any official move. We can't let them down!"

Originally it had been planned that after the ruins of the gold city had been cleaned with Tom's spectromarine selector, the site was to be turned over to United States supervision. The ancient city would be opened to tourists and scientific students of all countries. A foreign group which staked a claim might not be so generous.

"So far, there are no clues connecting Judson and Ebber with any known subversive organization," Ames remarked.

"They might be part of a gang that's merely after the gold," Tom conceded. "Even so, we'd better act fast."

Mr. Swift drummed his fingers thoughtfully. "How long would it take to build another spectromarine selector, son?"

"A few days." Tom's eyes flashed hopefully. "Can we afford it, Dad?"

"I'd say we can't afford *not* to, with so much at stake!" Mr. Swift smiled. "But it's strictly your project, Tom. I have my hands full with this new rocket contract bid."

"Right. I'll get on it immediately!"

Tom hurried back to the spacious modern office

which he shared with his father. There he beamed an electronic key at a file cabinet and took out the blueprints of his new invention. After studying the prints briefly, he made a rapid series of telephone calls, giving instructions to various sections of the plant. Within an hour the machine shop, forge, and electronic departments were at work on a new model of the de-organic-izer.

Tom hustled around by jet scooter, conferring with engineers and technicians and lending a guiding hand to the operations. By quitting time at five o'clock, he was thoroughly exhausted from the day's events.

Tom was clearing off his desk, prior to leaving for the day, when Ames walked into the office.

"Got a minute, skipper?"

"Sure. What's up, Harlan?"

"Just got some photos of Judson's partner from the FBI," Ames explained.

He handed over several prints, which Tom examined carefully. They were front and profile views of a gaunt-faced man with a beaklike nose. His scrawny neck and protuberant Adam's apple showed clearly why he had received his nickname.

"So this is Longneck Ebber." Tom memorized the man's features. "What's his record?"

"Everything from safecracking to felonious assault," Ames replied. "They say he's dangerous and plenty smart, skipper."

"Let's hope the FBI nails him soon!" Tom said.

He left the building a few minutes later and headed home in his sports car. Instead of taking the main road into Shopton, he followed a winding route that led through pleasant woodlands. Tom, who loved the outdoors, always found the scenery refreshing after a hard day's work at the plant.

"Man! That pine-scented air sure smells good," he thought, breathing in deeply.

On impulse Tom pulled to the side of the road and parked at a favorite spot. Getting out, he seated himself, parallel to the road, against the trunk of an oak tree, which overlooked a rocky ravine, dotted with wild flowers.

At that moment a metallic gray sedan sped by. Two men were in the front seat. Their heads were turned away, but Tom's attention was drawn by the sleek lines of the car as it shot past.

"A new Tioga," he noted admiringly. "That car has a real engine!"

Tom's thoughts soon turned to his own problems. What was behind Judson's sabotage of his new invention? Were other plotters at work to stop him from exploring the city of gold?

Tom was still deep in thought several minutes later when he was struck violently from behind. Blinding sparks of pain shot through his skull, then he blacked out!

CHAPTER III

THE WRECKED CAR

IT WAS nearing dinnertime at the Swift home. Sandra was setting the dining-room table while her mother basted the roast in the oven. The appetizing odor of beef wafted through the house.

"Mm! That smells heavenly!" Sandy exclaimed, coming back to the kitchen. "You are positively the best cook in seven counties, Mother!"

Mrs. Swift, a slender, attractive woman, gave her daughter a hug. "You're a flatterer, dear. But thanks!"

"I mean it—really," Sandy insisted. "Dad says you've spoiled us for any servant's cooking and he's right. It's your own fault!"

"I like cooking for my own family—it's a joy!" Mrs. Swift said. "That's why I do it."

As they proceeded with the preparations for dinner, Mr. Swift arrived home. After giving his wife and daughter a kiss, he reported that he had just come from a conference with Ned Newton on their government rocket contract bid. "Uncle Ned" was Phyl Newton's father and Tom Sr.'s lifelong friend. He managed the highly successful Swift Construction Company, which manufactured the Swifts' inventions.

"By the way, where's Tom?" Mr. Swift asked. "Not home yet?"

"No. In fact I'm getting worried," Mrs. Swift fretted. "When he phoned to tell us about the flight, he said he was famished and to expect him promptly."

Mr. Swift glanced at his watch. "Well, you know how absorbed Tom gets." The scientist smiled. "He's working on a new model of his invention to replace the one lost at sea."

Meanwhile, Sandy put the finishing touches to the table setting. The roast and vegetables were soon ready and the Swifts decided to eat.

Dusk was falling by the time dinner ended. Mr. Swift, remembering the sabotage plot against Tom's expedition, began to feel somewhat uneasy about his son. But he decided not to mention his fears to his wife and Sandy.

"I think perhaps I'll call the plant and jog Tom's memory," he said with a smile.

From the telephone alcove in the hallway he called Swift Enterprises on their private line. The night operator rang Tom's laboratory and then the double office in the main building. Neither call drew an answer. Next she paged the young inventor over the plant's public-address system—again without success.

"I'm sorry, sir," the operator reported. "Your son must have left."

"All right. Thank you." Mr. Swift hung up, then called Bud at the house in the Shopton suburbs where he boarded with several of the young engineers from Enterprises. Bud's own family lived in San Francisco.

"Sorry to disturb you, Bud," the scientist said pleasantly when the young copilot answered the phone. "Tom hasn't come home yet and I wondered if you'd seen him."

"Why, no, sir. Not since this afternoon," Bud replied. "Think there's something wrong?"

Mr. Swift hesitated. "I hope not, but frankly I'm not sure."

Bud sensed Mr. Swift's uneasiness and his desire not to alarm the other members of his family. "Mr. Swift, let me get hold of Harlan Ames. I'll call back as soon as possible."

"Thanks, Bud!"

Mr. Swift returned to the living room, trying to conceal his inner concern. But his wife's eyes met those of the inventor in a worried look.

"Dear, is Tom all right?" she asked anxiously.

Her husband replied reassuringly, "So far I can't reach him, but we'll no doubt hear from him soon, Mary."

All three waited worriedly in the big comfortable living room. Tense moments crept by. When the telephone rang, Mr. Swift sprang up immediately to answer it.

"This is Bud," the caller said. "I talked to Ames and he thinks we'd better start a search. Would it upset Mrs. Swift if we dropped over and talked about it?"

"Come ahead, Bud!" the scientist replied.

A few minutes later Bud's convertible pulled up the graveled drive. Arv Hanson, the hulking six-footer who hand-tooled the delicate scale models of all the Swifts' inventions, was with him. Ames arrived shortly afterward, bringing Slim Davis and Hank Sterling, the quiet-spoken, hard-fisted chief patternmaking engineer of Enterprises.

"No news?" Mr. Swift greeted the new arrivals at the front door.

"Not yet," Ames replied, then whispered, "We're afraid that Tom's absence may be connected with the arrest today of Judson." The security chief walked into the living room and was greeted by Tom's mother and sister. He asked, "Can you think of any errand that might have taken Tom out of his way?"

The Swifts shook their heads to both questions.

"Then," Ames went on, "we'd better divide into search parties and cover every route Tom may have taken from the plant. If that doesn't turn up any clues, we'll call the police."

After a hurried conference to settle their plan of action, Bud took off in his convertible with Arv Hanson. Ames went with Slim Davis. Mr. Swift followed in his own car, accompanied by Hank Sterling.

Fanning out through Shopton, they questioned traffic policemen, news vendors, and gas station operators—anyone who might have noticed the young inventor's familiar custom-built sports car.

Mr. Swift then drove over the tree-shaded dirt lane which he and Tom sometimes used when they felt like walking home. The other two cars took the main highway which led from the outskirts of Shopton past Enterprises. All reported failure when they met at the plant.

Mr. Swift was tight-lipped but calm. "I believe Tom has occasionally taken that winding road around Lake Carlopa," he recalled. "Suppose we give it a try."

The three cars set off together, using spotlights to illumine both sides of the wooded road. All three vehicles were fitted with the short-range, two-way radios used for communicating with Enterprises.

Ames was in the lead. Suddenly his car swerved toward the dirt shoulder and braked to a halt.

"Hold it!" he radioed. "This may be our clue!"

The others braked their cars to a stop and leaped out. Ames's spotlight showed tire tracks and an oil stain where a car had parked. Crushed

underbrush pointed a further route where the
car had later been pushed or driven toward the
nearby ravine.

Mr. Swift went pale. "Tire tracks from
Tom's car!" he murmured. "I recognize the tread
pattern."

Hank Sterling gripped Mr. Swift's arm. "Maybe
you'd better stay here."

But with his son's fate in question, nothing
could stop the scientist. All five grabbed powerful flashlights from the cars and hurried to investigate the ravine.

"Oh, *no!*" A tense cry escaped Bud's lips. Tom's
sports car lay overturned among the tangled underbrush below!

Sick with fear, the searchers scrambled down
the sloping bank. But a fresh shock was in store.
The car was empty!

"Maybe Tom was dazed by the accident," Bud
suggested hopefully. "Perhaps he's wandering
around somewhere close by!"

"That's an idea!" Arv agreed. "Let's look!"

Mr. Swift scarcely trusted himself to speak.
As the others spread out, shouting Tom's name,
Ames offered another suggestion.

"It's just possible he was picked up by some
motorist," the security chief murmured. "Stay
here, sir, and I'll check."

Dashing back to his car, Ames called Enterprises
on his radio and requested a patch line so he

could use the telephone. He called Shopton's hospitals and clinics, but none had admitted a recent accident victim answering Tom's description.

When Ames rejoined Mr. Swift, he saw lights moving about the hillside beyond the ravine as the other searchers widened their area.

"Tom! . . . Tom Swift!" Their repeated calls echoed through the darkness.

Suddenly a yell from Bud electrified his companions. Within moments all of them had rushed to his side. Ames arrived last and gave a startled gasp.

Tom lay unconscious on the ground. The glow of their flashlights revealed a crudely printed note pinned to his T shirt. It read:

> YOU'VE HAD YOUR WARNING. NOW KEEP YOUR MOUTH SHUT AND STAY IN SHOPTON! TRY LEAVING ON ANOTHER EXPEDITION AND YOU'LL NEVER MAKE IT ALIVE!

Mr. Swift, grim-faced, knelt beside his son and slipped one arm under Tom's shoulders.

"He's had a blow on the head," he muttered after a quick examination. "Let's hope it isn't serious."

Bud, overjoyed at finding his pal, ran back to the cars. He returned quickly, bringing a first-aid kit and a canteen of water. He gave Tom a few drops of spirits of ammonia in water, after the young inventor began to revive.

"Easy, son," his father said. "You've had a bad clout on the head, so lie still for a bit."

Tom moaned and opened his eyes. "Oo-o-oh! What hit me?" Then he forced a wan smile as he

recognized the faces bending over him. Presently Tom recovered enough to tell what had happened.

"Did you get any glimpse of the person or persons who hit you?" Ames inquired.

Tom shook his head painfully. "No."

When Ames showed him the threatening note, Tom read it and frowned thoughtfully.

"This is only a hunch, Harlan, but two men passed in a car right after I stopped and got out. Their faces were turned away, so I can't tell you what they looked like. Anyway, possibly they could give you a lead to the thugs. Their car was a brand-new Tioga sedan—metallic gray color. See if you can trace it."

The security chief promised to do so.

"Another thing," Tom added, "you might check the source of that note paper. It looks as if it came from an office memo pad."

Ames nodded. "Good thought, Tom. And I'll test it under your electronic retroscope, too."

Hank and Slim carried the young inventor back to his father's car on an improvised stretcher. Mr. Swift rushed him home, while Bud sped off to bring Doc Simpson, the young Enterprises plant physician. The others remained behind to tackle the job of salvaging Tom's sports car.

When Doc Simpson arrived at the house, he examined Tom and found no signs of concussion.

"Rest and some sound sleep will be the only treatment necessary," Doc Simpson assured Mrs. Swift and Sandy, who gave grateful sighs of relief.

By morning Tom felt fine and was bursting with energy. He greeted his mother and sister with a smile as he sat down to a late breakfast. Mr. Swift had already left.

"Please stay at home today," Mrs. Swift urged anxiously.

"Can't, Mom! Honestly!" Tom grinned and hugged her. "But I promise I'll—"

He broke off as the telephone rang. Tom went to answer it. Harlan Ames was calling.

After asking Tom how he felt, Ames reported, "That was a good hunch of yours about the paper coming from an office memo. I traced it through the manufacturer to the Tioga Motor Company."

Tom listened with keen interest as the security chief added, "And here's some more news, skipper!"

CHAPTER IV

FEEDBACK FLAW

AMES explained to Tom that he had called the manager of the Tioga Motor Company in Detroit.

"When I mentioned Judson and Ebber," Ames went on, "he told me that Joe Judson had been working there as a bookkeeper. But he quit last week—and two days later they discovered a big shortage in his accounts!"

Tom whistled in amazement. "You mean they hired him even though he had served time as an embezzler?"

Ames explained that Judson had been frank about his prison record and had managed to convince the company that he intended to go straight.

"But after hearing the news about Judson's latest arrest, the manager is sure he's the man responsible for the shortage."

"What does Judson say about it?" Tom asked. "Have you talked to him since yesterday?"

The security chief reported that he had just come back from the Shopton jail after questioning the prisoner for a second time.

"But it was a waste of effort," Ames concluded. "Judson still won't talk."

Tom mulled this over. "Hmm. Maybe if Long-neck Ebber is found, it'll solve the mystery."

"I hope so," Ames said glumly. "But the FBI has no lead on him yet."

Shortly after Ames's call, Doc Simpson arrived at the house. He firmly ordered Tom back to bed.

"No use pleading, skipper," the medic said. "That was a nasty blow you got. If you overdo things, it could have some aftereffects. Now you stay in bed and take it easy—at least for today."

Tom fumed but complied. Sandy did her best to keep her brother amused throughout the day. But it was hard for someone as keen and active as Tom to stay cooped up like an invalid when he felt well and sunshine was pouring through the windows. Besides, there was so much work to be done!

Fortunately, Bud stopped during the afternoon, bringing Phyllis Newton in his red convertible. Phyl was Tom's favorite date.

"What a break!" he exclaimed with a grin.

Phyl's brown eyes twinkled as she produced a gift she and Bud had brought. "I guess that blow on the head wasn't too serious, Tom, but here— get well soon!"

She held out a tempting basket of glazed fruits and other delicacies.

"Wow! This is worth having to stay in bed for!" Tom chuckled with delight at the girl's thoughtfulness. "Thanks a million, you two!"

"We'll help you eat it," Sandy volunteered.

Tom tore off the cellophane and passed the basket around. As they nibbled the fruits, Phyl asked how Tom had been passing the time.

"He beat me so often at chess that he got bored," Sandy replied. She giggled. "Then he started working out theorems in rubber-sheet geometry."

"Good night, what's that?" Bud asked.

"Don't ask me!" Sandy retorted mischievously. "He says it deals with such problems as whether the hole is inside or outside of a doughnut."

Tom laughed at Bud's popeyed stare.

"The real name for it is topology. It's a little tough to explain."

"Okay! Don't bother," said Bud hastily.

"Then explain something to me," Phyl begged laughingly. "How does your new invention, the spectromarine selector, alias de-organic-izer, alias organ, work? You told me about the vacuum part, but you hadn't yet perfected the rest of it. Something to do with 'cracking,' I think," she added, frowning.

"Oh, you mean the S-Co. Right name semoreco," Tom replied. "It stands for selective molecule recombiner. The idea is somewhat like petroleum cracking in a refinery—"

"Or the cracking of my head when I try to follow Professor Einstein here," Bud quipped.

Tom grinned. "There's a simpler way, pal. I'll be glad to oblige any time."

"Okay, okay!" Bud ducked. "Excuse the interruption, please!"

"By 'cracking,'" Tom went on, "I mean that the semoreco breaks down the big organic molecules of sea growths or other masses which have to be cleaned away from objects. Here, I'll show you."

The young inventor went to his bedroom closet and brought out a miniature pilot model of his de-organic-izer.

"Hey! Pretty keen!" Bud exclaimed. They were all amazed by the gleaming, toylike device.

Tom pointed out the operator's platform, mounted on tractor treads, and the control pedestal with a cannonlike tube sticking out in front.

"This tube is the hydraulic unit," Tom said. "And up front here is the infrared device for heating the moisture when you begin cleaning."

"That's what you were telling Chow about on the plane?" Bud put in.

"Right. It's hooked up with the localator vacuum producer, or LVP."

Tom also pointed out another device at the front. It was shaped like a funnel and contained a maze of tiny coils and transistors.

"This is the semoreco unit," he went on. "Instead of cracking the molecules by heat, this does the same thing electronically. Then it recombines, or in a sense selects, the atoms of the various elements to form water, carbon dioxide, or useful compounds."

These, Tom explained, were drawn off through the hydraulic tube into storage tanks at the rear. The semoreco control panel, studded with tiny levers and dials, was just behind the operator.

"This little model actually works?" Phyl asked in amazement.

"Sure," Tom turned to Bud with a grin. "Like a little hair off the top, pal?"

"Please! Don't experiment on me, Professor!"

Phyl held up her leather purse with silver initials. "These need shining," she said playfully. "Could your machine remove the tarnish?"

"No sooner said than done, madame!"

Tom aimed the organ at the metal initials. Then he flicked on the power, provided by a miniature solar battery, and turned a dial.

Phyl and Sandy gasped as the tarnish disappeared like magic. But their amazement quickly turned to dismay as the initials too began to vanish. Before Tom could turn off the machine, even the leather was partly eaten away!

"It's ruined!" Sandy groaned.

Tom, red-faced, hastily apologized.

"Don't worry," Phyl said good-naturedly. "It

was an old purse, anyhow. But what happened?"

Tom explained that he had adjusted the machine to remove tarnish, a sulfide compound. But the selector circuit, by a feedback action, had also ordered the machine to remove the metal.

"There's sulfur in the leather, too," he added. "So the organ took part of *that* off!"

"Just a slight slip-up." Bud grinned.

"A slip-up that could cause plenty of damage," Tom admitted ruefully. "I'll buy you a new purse, Phyl, and let's say this one went for the cause of science. At least it showed me a flaw in my machine that needs correcting!"

The next morning Doc Simpson examined Tom again. This time he pronounced the young inventor well enough to return to work. Tom gave a whoop of relief.

As soon as he arrived at the plant, Tom made a quick tour of the various departments to check progress on his new de-organic-izer. Luckily there was still time to make changes in the S-Co unit. On this he went to confer with Art Wiltessa, a brilliant young engineer in the plant's machine shop.

"What's the deal, skipper?" asked Art, who had supervised the production of many of Tom's projects from blueprints to working model.

Tom explained the flaw that had spoiled his demonstration on Phyl's purse. "I think I have the answer," he added.

Pulling out pencil and paper, Tom sketched a feedback-control circuit which he had worked out in his mind overnight. Its purpose was to prevent the compounds in the object being cleaned from affecting the selection of elements to be removed.

"Pretty slick," Art commented. "And we can add that easily before the unit's assembled."

"Thanks, Art." Tom slapped him on the back. "I hate to slow up your schedule, but we want all the bugs ironed out before tackling those Atlantis ruins."

Tom, nevertheless, determined to make good use of the time while waiting for the new organ to be completed. Therefore, at lunchtime, he proposed to his father and Harlan Ames that he make a quick scouting trip to the undersea site.

"It'll give us a chance to find out whether or not any other expedition has shown up to stake out a claim on the city of gold," Tom explained.

Mr. Swift frowned doubtfully. "Is that wise, son? The sabotage plot and that threat against your life show that you're up against some clever, ruthless enemies."

Ames concurred. "And you might be followed. Once they learn the location, they might beat us to the draw with an expedition."

But Tom felt sure that the secret of the undersea site was already known. "Otherwise," he argued, "our enemies would have postponed their sabotage scheme until Judson had a chance to spy out the place. What they're trying to do is keep me away!"

Both Ames and Mr. Swift saw the logic in Tom's theory, and agreed to the young inventor's proposal. Accordingly, Tom and Bud flew to Fearing Island. This small, barren stretch of sand dunes and scrubgrass off the Atlantic Coast had been converted into the Swifts' top-secret rocket-testing laboratory. It was now the supply base for Tom's space station, as well as the launching area for his expeditions into outer space.

After clearing with the tower, the boys landed on the island and sped by jeep to the seacopter hangar. A crew was standing by, ready for a trip in the *Sea Hound.*

"Your helicopter-submarine is all slicked up," Bud remarked, after the boys had greeted the crew members.

Tom took his place at the controls, with Bud beside him in the copilot's seat. He flicked on the atomic reactor, shooting steam to the turbines which spun the enclosed horizontal rotor. With a purring hum the seacopter soared skyward.

High over the ocean, Tom cut in the forward jet tubes and the *Sea Hound* went streaking off to the north.

"Hey! Where are we heading?" Bud questioned with a look of surprise. "The North Pole?"

Tom grinned and shook his head. "Just a slight precaution to mislead any spies."

He flew northward for almost a hundred miles, then gradually altered course toward the southeast. Far out over the mid-Atlantic, Tom brought the seacopter down and submerged. But even below the surface, he zigzagged warily.

"Any blips?" he asked the crewman who was scanning the sonarscope.

"All clear, skipper!"

Finally convinced they were free of any possible pursuers, Tom laid a course for the sunken city in the South Atlantic. Hours went by as he and Bud watched the deep-sea fishes and other colorful ocean life pass by through the greenish waters outside the quartz window of the cabin.

At last a signal light flashed on the automatic navigator. They were now directly over the city of gold, two miles down. Tom shoved the control wheel forward and the *Sea Hound* plunged toward the ocean bottom.

The waters darkened and gradually became pitch black. Tom switched on the powerful undersea searchlight. Presently the rugged crags of the Atlantic Ridge conformation came into view. Moments later, a gentle thud announced that they had settled on the sea floor.

"Look!" Bud gave a startled gasp and pointed out the cabin window.

Dead ahead, in the full glare of the seacopter's beam, lay a strange submarine!

CHAPTER V

A GHASTLY HULK

THE mysterious craft remained motionless, betraying no sign of hostile intent. Its crew, if any, seemed unaware of the *Sea Hound's* presence and gave no response when Tom called the submarine over the sonarphone.

"What do you make of it, skipper?" Bud asked with a puzzled scowl.

Tom was equally baffled. "You've got me, Bud. I can't even guess its nationality."

He pulled out a copy of *Jane's Fighting Ships,* which he kept with his navigation charts, and flipped through its pages. But he found no submarines pictured with lines like those of the unknown craft.

"Must be some new type that's been kept top secret," Tom muttered. "Especially to be operating at this depth!" He shot Bud a quizzical glance. "Are you game to pay 'em a visit?"

"In Fat Man suits?" Bud grinned. "Sure, why

not? Boy, will they be surprised to see *us* at their front door!"

The Fat Men were deep-sea escape suits, invented by Tom during his jetmarine adventure with undersea pirates. Shaped like steel eggs, the suits were balanced by an inside gyrobrain and had mechanical pantograph arms and legs.

Tom and Bud each squirmed into a suit and clamped shut the quartz-glass view plate. Moments later, the queer-looking steel monsters emerged through the *Sea Hound's* outer hatch.

The crewmen tending the controls watched tensely through the cabin windows as Tom and Bud waddled forward through the undersea murk. Each suit carried its own spotlight. At this depth the Fat Men were under extreme pressure and bone-chilling temperature. But inside, Tom and Bud were perfectly comfortable on their operator's seats, working the air-propulsion jets.

Reaching the mystery submarine, Tom manipulated his Fat Man's arm controls to rap on the hull. Repeated knocks brought no response.

"Maybe there's no one aboard," Bud remarked over his suit's sonarphone.

"Just what I'm thinking." Tom's face, seen through his quartz view pane, bore a puzzled frown. "It may even be a derelict."

"So what do we do now?"

"Let's open 'er up and find out."

Bud was secretly fearful that the submarine's

occupants might have set this trap to capture Tom. But he said nothing and trusted to his pal's judgment.

The boys navigated their steel eggs back across the ocean floor to their own craft. Then Tom steered the *Sea Hound* close alongside the other submarine, so that the hose of an undersea cutting torch could be run out through the air lock.

Again the boys left through the hatch in their Fat Man suits. With his pantograph arms, Tom adjusted the nozzle and guided the torch as its sizzling jet of flame bit into the steel lip of the strange craft's hatch. Presently he had cut a hole big enough to insert a forcing tool.

"Okay, let's get a crowbar in here," he told Bud over the sonarphone.

The two boys inserted the huge crowbar and began prying at the hatch. Fortunately, their Fat Men's arms were capable of exerting powerful leverage. Under repeated efforts, the hatch finally yielded and slid back.

Once inside the ship's air lock, Tom quickly mastered the opening mechanism of the inner door. He and Bud expected the sea water to surge in explosively. Instead, a gruesome surprise awaited the boys as they stepped inside. The submarine was already flooded!

"Oh!" both boys cried out and their faces went pale. Human skeletons floated among the debris of the craft's interior! A few tattered shreds of uniform clung to the bones, but not enough to establish any identity.

Tom averted his eyes. "Now we know why they didn't answer. We'd better look around for clues, Bud—but let's make it fast!"

Hastily the boys probed through the swamped compartments. The submarine had been powered by atomic reactors. But neither the gauge dials nor any of the machinery bore a manufacturer's trademark.

"Not a hint of any nationality," Bud muttered. "Do you suppose they left off all markings on purpose?"

Tom doubted this. "It's more likely," he conjectured, "that the sub was an experimental job —practically all hand-built."

As they returned to the air lock, a bin of special tools caught Tom's eye. They included scrapers, wire brushes, and what looked like small portable jet-blasting devices.

"Oh—oh! Maybe this gear explains the sub's mission," he murmured over his sonarphone.

"Meaning what?" Bud asked.

"It may have been intended for cleaning off those undersea ruins." Tom picked up several of the tools and urged Bud to do likewise. "I'll test them when we get back to Shopton," he added. "They might provide a clue."

Tom propelled his Fat Man out through the

air lock. The *Sea Hound,* following orders, had withdrawn to a safe distance in case of any surprise developments aboard the mystery undersea craft.

Tom started back through the murk of the ocean bottom. He was halfway to the seacopter when a cry came over his sonarphone:

"Skipper! Help!"

Tom wheeled around in his steel egg. A chill of fear went through his veins. Bud was trapped just outside the mystery submarine's air lock! Apparently, in leaving, he had accidentally tripped the closing mechanism. The heavy hatch had slid shut, pinning one leg of his Fat Man suit inside the submarine!

Gunning his air jet, Tom propelled himself back toward the submarine. His brain was working fast. Without a crowbar, could his Fat Man arms pry the hatch enough to free Bud?

One glance at Bud's face told him the danger was acute.

"My suit's leaking!" Bud signaled over his sonarphone. His eyes were bleak with fear.

Tom guessed the reason. The strain caused by trying to wrench loose the mechanical leg must have cracked the hydroseal at the socket joint! This seal around the tiny servoaction lead controlled the leg's pantograph movements.

"Easy, pal!" Tom tried to keep his voice calm.

"Skipper! Help!" Bud cried out

"Don't put any more strain on that leg joint and I'll have you free in a jiffy!"

Tom inserted the claws of his Fat Man's arms in the hatch opening. Slowly he applied leverage. His heart leaped as he noticed the hatch beginning to give slightly.

"Hurry, Tom!"

In a second Bud was able to pull the leg free. Tom veered around in his Fat Man. Then he saw that what had caused Bud's yell was not his leaking suit. A weird luminescent sea creature was darting toward them!

Half fish, half sea serpent, the monster glowed with an eerie bluish light. It was at least fifty feet long!

"Try to scare him off!" Tom signaled. He slashed the water with his Fat Man arms and Bud followed suit.

But the monster showed no signs of fear. Its protuberant eyes, extended on stalks, glared at them ferociously. Its powerful jaws gaped open, revealing rows of spiky teeth.

"Watch it!" Bud gasped. "The thing's starting to coil!"

Like a huge boa constrictor, the slithering creature was attempting to wrap itself around their Fat Men's limbs. If the serpent was as powerful as it looked, it might easily damage or wrench off one of the mechanical arms or legs. The resulting leakage could be fatal to Tom or Bud.

"Claw at him!" Tom advised.

Both boys manipulated their arm controls frantically. The steel claws bit into the creature's leather-tough flesh.

Meanwhile, the crewmen aboard the *Sea Hound* had observed the boys' plight and sent the sea-copter racing toward the scene of action. But the horrified watchers could do little to assist. They tried scaring the creature away without injuring Tom and Bud, but had no luck.

The serpent was now thrashing about wildly, churning up clouds of murky froth. It was suffering severe punishment as the Fat Men's claws tore jagged rips in its flesh. Then suddenly the creature relaxed its coils and went darting off beyond range of their lights.

"Good grief! What a nightmare!" Bud gasped weakly.

"Get aboard fast!" Tom signaled.

Quickly they made their way into the *Sea Hound's* air lock. Bud, shivering and blue with chill from the seepage of the icy water, climbed out of his suit. But he soon recovered after changing into dry clothes and gulping down several mugs of hot cocoa from the galley.

"Wow!" Bud gave a pent-up sigh of relief. "Say, I wonder if that's the monster which caused all the ancient stories about sea serpents!"

Tom shrugged. "Who knows? Science hasn't yet studied the forms of sea life as far down as we are.

Most of the creatures would explode if brought to the surface."

Taking his place at the controls once more, he covered the distance along the main section of the city of gold. There was no sign of activity.

"What now, explorer boy?" Bud asked.

"Home—fast," Tom replied tersely.

He cut the rotors, permitting the *Sea Hound* to rise to the surface. He was eager to radio a report to Enterprises but decided against it for fear the broadcast might give away their position.

Reversing the blade pitch for helicopter action, Tom gunned the atomic turbine. The *Sea Hound* soared gracefully above the ocean. Then, as he cut in the forward jets, the seacopter streaked back toward the United States.

A pleasant surprise awaited the travelers when they landed at Fearing Island. Mr. Swift had flown out to the rocket base for a conference in connection with his government contract bid. Tom poured out the story of the lost submarine.

The elder scientist's face wore a grim frown. "I wonder if it was just an accident that the sub sank at that particular spot? Or were those men planning to explore the city of gold?"

"Good question." Tom considered his father's words thoughtfully. "I suspect the latter, judging from certain tools we found aboard. If I can determine where they came from, it may give us a clue."

Having completed his business on Fearing, Mr.

Swift flew back to Shopton with Tom and Bud. En route he informed them that the Swift Construction Company, as lowest bidder, had been awarded a government contract to produce a number of rockets based on his own improved design.

"Wonderful, Dad!" Tom exclaimed. "I was sure you'd win out." Bud added his congratulations.

But Mr. Swift shook his head worriedly. "My troubles are just beginning," he told the boys. "The terms call for faster production than I'd anticipated. Frankly, I'm afraid we can't deliver all the rockets on time—in fact, we'll be doing well to turn out half that number!"

"Why not use our facilities at Enterprises?" Tom urged. "Put everyone on the project!"

"It's not manpower," his father explained. "It's a matter of obtaining a prompt supply of the rare metals I need. I hate to fall down on the job when our country needs those rockets so urgently. But I've exhausted every means I know of to get those metals."

With a glum sigh, Mr. Swift added, "It looks as if the job may have to go to the next lowest bidder."

CHAPTER VI

LABORATORY CLUE

"WHAT *are* the rare metals you need, sir?" Bud asked curiously.

"Some of them should be familiar to you, Bud." Mr. Swift smiled. "After all, you and Tom discovered the quarry where they're mined."

"Dad's talking about those so-called rare earths we found in New Guinea," Tom put in. "Remember?"

"Oh sure," Bud recalled. "You mean those metals with the jawbreaking names, like—well, like praseo-something."

Tom grinned. "Praseodymium. Yes, that's one of them, Bud. Anyhow, Dad's been using several of those rare-earth elements to produce the light-weight, high-strength alloy he needs for the air frame of his new rockets."

"Plus a few other rare metals," Mr. Swift added, "including Lunite from the phantom satellite."

The scientist went on to explain that the job of obtaining and combining these metals into a complex alloy had led to many production headaches.

"If only I could find a new metal with the right properties!" Mr. Swift mused wistfully. "Perhaps a metal which I could combine with plain magnesium. That would not only cut down the cost of the rockets but greatly speed up production!"

"What you need is a real atomic-age jet metal!" Bud quipped. "Let's see. You could call the new alloy 'atom-something.' Atomeron! How about that?"

"Good name." Mr. Swift grinned. "But first I'll have to find the right ingredient."

"Nothing to it, Dad," Tom said jokingly. "Just leave that to Barclay and Swift—Atomic-Age Prospectors, Incorporated!"

"Fine! But make it soon, please. Remember, that whole government contract has to be filled in six months."

All three laughed, somewhat lightening the gloomy atmosphere. Secretly Tom wished that he could find the solution to his father's problem.

The flight back to Shopton took only a short time. As soon as the jet plane landed at Enterprises, Mr. Swift hurried to his office in the main building.

"We'll go to the lab with these tools we took from the sunken sub," Tom said, jumping into a jeep.

The boys drove to the young inventor's glass-walled private laboratory. The airy, spacious building—flooded now with midafternoon sunshine—contained a bewildering array of scientific equipment. Almost every development of modern research, from an antigravity bubble to a helium cryostat, could be found within its walls. It was here that Tom carried on the exciting experiments which led to his amazing inventions.

"What's first on the program?" Bud asked as they dumped the tools onto a workbench.

"I'll test this stuff with my retroscope camera," Tom replied. "It may show up a manufacturer's name or trade-mark. If not, I'll do a spectrographic analysis."

Tom's electronic retroscope had had its first tryout a few months earlier when he had used it to reveal some long-eroded Mayan temple carvings in Mexico. The device worked by tracing out the inner pattern of radioactive aging. This pattern was like an invisible "carbon copy" of the original markings on the object being tested.

"Lights! Action! Camera!" Bud quipped as Tom switched on the equipment.

The young inventor grinned and focused the scanning unit on the first tool—a hand scraper. Like the others, it showed signs of hard use, no doubt from years of removing paint from other ships.

Tom turned several dials. The retroscope

hummed into action. Presently a symbol showed up on the oscilloscope screen of the reproducing unit. It was a triangle containing the letter V.

"What's that?" Bud asked. "The manufacturer's trade-mark?"

Tom nodded, frowning thoughtfully. "I imagine so, but I can't place it offhand. . . . Hmm. Wait a minute."

Suddenly he snapped his fingers. A worried look came over his face.

"Got it?" Bud inquired.

"I think so. But I sure hope I'm wrong!"

Tom said nothing more as he tested the other hand tools. All bore the same symbol. The portable jet blasters, however, showed no markings of any kind under the retroscope.

"I guess these jobs aren't production items," Tom muttered. "They were probably specially designed and assembled for that sub's undersea expedition."

"Okay, but what about those triangle-V symbols?" Bud asked. "Going to keep it a secret?"

"Give me a few minutes more," Tom said. "Then I'll know for sure."

Switching on a power tool, he sliced a piece of metal off one of the scrapers. Next, he placed the sample in a Swift spectrograph and pressed a button. A surge of electromagnetic energy shot through the metal, heating it to glowing incandescence. A moment later Tom pulled out the chart and studied the recorded spectrum. He then fed this chart into a computer, which, in a matter of seconds, compared it to all known types of steel.

"Well?" Bud watched his friend's expression. "Is it what you expected?"

Tom nodded, tight-lipped. "This analysis proves it." Looking up, he added, "Ever hear of the Varda steelworks?"

"Not that I recall. Is that what the V symbol stands for?"

"Right. Varda produces some of the finest tool steel in the world, alloyed to their own special formula. Their trade-mark used to be well known. Then another country took over the plant—working through one of their satellite puppet governments—and shut off all export."

"What country?" Bud still looked puzzled.

"Brungaria," Tom replied grimly.

Bud gave a whistle of dismay. Brungarian political factions had long been hostile to the free world, and their agents had tried repeatedly to foil Tom's scientific exploits. They had even resorted to force and fraud to stop Tom's space expedition from claiming the phantom satellite, Nestria, for the United States.

"Good night!" Bud muttered. "Then if these tools were manufactured by Varda, that submarine was probably Brungarian!"

"Exactly." Tom paced up and down the laboratory, a look of great concern on his lean young face. "Bud, this discovery is something to worry about."

"You're telling me!" Bud slumped down angrily on a laboratory stool. "Judging from the stunts their scientists have pulled before, those babies won't stop at anything! But how did they find out about the city of gold?"

"I wish I knew!" Tom ran his fingers through his blond crew cut. "Another thing I'd like to know is whether Judson and Longneck Ebber are tied up with them."

"I sure wouldn't put it past those rats!" Bud growled.

"Never mind, buckaroos!" boomed a cheerful voice. "Jest stow your troubles an' tie into this grub!"

Looking up, the boys saw Chow Winkler in the laboratory doorway. He was balancing a lunch tray on one hand.

"Brand my ranch rockets! 'Bout time you fellows had *good* food after that cruise," the ex-ranch cook declared. "An' remember," he added, "bad temper can be plumb poisonous to a man's digestion!"

Tom and Bud grinned. The Texan was sporting another of his loud cowboy outfits, including a lemon-yellow shirt and fancy beaded vest.

"Look at those new boots!" Bud exclaimed.

Chow's latest footgear, high-heeled as usual, was

of shiny patent leather, decorated in a white curl-icue design.

"Ain't they jim-dandies?" Chow chuckled proudly as he hoisted the tray aloft with a flourish and started a cowboy jig. The next instant he lost his balance and landed with a thud, followed by the crash of dishes. The boys made sure he had not hurt himself, then burst into laughter.

"Wal, what's so funny?" Chow roared.

"Ah-ah!" Bud wagged his finger scoldingly. "Remember what you said about bad temper spoiling a man's digestion!"

Still chuckling, Tom and Bud helped the plump Texan to his feet. He glowered for a moment, then his leathery face relaxed into a sheepish grin. "Brand my tumblin' saddlebags, reckon I must 'a' looked kind o' funny at that," he conceded good-naturedly.

Looking down at his stained vest and shirt front, he added mournfully, "It ain't the fall I mind so much as this hot soup on my new outfit!"

To soothe his feelings, Tom and Bud took over the job of mopping up. Twenty minutes later Chow returned with a fresh tray of food. Both boys ate ravenously.

As Tom munched a hot chicken sandwich, he said, "Guess I'd better call Ames and give him a report on these tools."

As soon as he finished eating, he picked up the telephone and dialed the security department.

Ames, who had received a radio report from Fearing Island about the sunken submarine, was alarmed by this latest clue.

"So we're up against the Brungarians again!" the security chief grumbled.

"It looks that way," Tom agreed.

Ames, too, immediately suspected that these old enemies of the Swifts might have hired Judson and Ebber to carry out the sabotage plot. He suggested to Tom that they pay another visit to the Shopton jail and quiz Judson again.

"Good idea, Harlan," Tom said.

A few minutes later the security chief pulled up in a car outside the laboratory. Tom and Bud piled in beside him and they drove to town. At police headquarters they talked to Chief Slater for a few moments. Then a turnkey admitted them to Judson's cell.

The prisoner was lounging on his bunk, smoking a cigarette. He eyed his three visitors mockingly.

"Why don't you guys give up?" he jeered. "I'm not talking, so save your breath!"

Tom eyed the man coldly. He decided to try catching Judson off guard. "In other words," he snapped, "you'd rather sell out your own country to the Brungarians!"

Judson stiffened as if he had received an electric shock. "How did you know I—"

Then his voice broke off.

CHAPTER VII

THE CARNIVAL SUSPECT

"GO ON! Talk!" Ames ordered the prisoner. But Judson's jaw clamped shut. He slumped back sullenly on his cot.

"Didn't know we were wise to your Brungarian deal, eh?" Tom needled the ex-convict, hoping to provoke another outburst. "Well, get this, Judson. You're nothing but a stooge so far as they're concerned, and now they've left you holding the bag!"

"What'll he get for treason and sabotage?" Bud asked, sensing Tom's strategy.

"It could be life," Ames replied emphatically, "unless he's smart enough to talk."

Judson glared at the trio. "I told you guys you're wasting your breath," he snarled. "So clear out and leave me alone!"

Ames hammered more questions at the prisoner, but he refused to utter another word. At last, Tom and his two companions gave up.

Chief Slater spoke to them as they left the cell block. "Any luck?"

Tom reported Judson's startled reaction when accused of working for the Brungarians.

Slater was impressed. "Sounds as if that's the best lead to work on, all right. I'll pass the word along to the FBI."

"Do that," Ames said. "And I'll notify the State Department and Central Intelligence."

Somewhat glumly, the group drove back to Enterprises. At four-thirty that afternoon Sandy telephoned her brother. She asked Tom to bring Bud Barclay home to dinner that evening.

"Phyl and I are expecting you," she said.

Tom grinned into the telephone. "Okay, Sis."

Chuckling, he called Bud at the experimental hangar. The copilot accepted.

"What's up?" Bud asked.

"I'm not sure," Tom replied. "But I have a hunch that Phyl and Sandy are going to tell us that we don't date them often enough."

Bud stopped at Tom's laboratory soon after five o'clock. When they arrived at the Swift home, Sandy and Phyl greeted them sweetly. Gay chatter prevailed at dinner, but afterward, the two girls cornered Tom and Bud in the living room.

"How's that new model of your invention coming, Tom?" Phyl asked casually.

"I'm hoping it'll be finished by Monday," Tom replied.

"Then I don't suppose you'll be taking off for the sunken city over the week end?"

"Not a chance. We'll probably work Saturday, though."

"Don't try to wiggle out!" Sandy put in, her blue eyes sparkling. "If you two boys aren't leaving over the week end, then there's no reason why you can't come out on a double date with Phyl and me!"

"Oh—oh!" Bud looked at Tom. "You were right, pal. This whole dinner was a put-up job. And here I thought they were feeding us out of the kindness of their hearts!"

"A fine answer," Sandy pouted. "Is there something wrong with us, Phyl?"

Phyl's long dark lashes drooped sadly as she smothered a giggle. "It's no use, Sandy. I guess we're just not their type."

"Oh well." Sandy shrugged mischievously. "If they have to work so hard all the time, maybe we better find ourselves other dates."

This brought a quick reaction from Bud. "Hey, none of that!" he protested. "Maybe we could manage to break away. What's up?"

Sandy and Phyl refused to reveal their plans. Tom's sister said that they would meet the boys at the plant Saturday at noon.

The next day was Friday. Both Tom and Bud had busy schedules and saw little of each other. But promptly at quarter to twelve on Saturday,

Bud hurried into Tom's laboratory. The boys washed, changed into white shirts, sports jackets, and slacks, and then waited for Sandy and Phyl to appear. They were expecting the girls to drive up outside the laboratory building.

Instead, a call came over the loud-speaker: "Tom Swift and Bud Barclay, please report to the airfield!"

The two friends hurried to a jeep and sped to the field. To their amazement, the girls were parked on an airstrip in a Pigeon Special, one of the sleek private planes produced by the Swift Construction Company. Sandy, an excellent pilot, often flew one for pleasure or demonstrated the craft to prospective customers.

"Hey, what's this?" Bud exclaimed, as he and Tom hopped out of the jeep. "A test flight? I thought we were all set for a date!"

"We are." Sandy's blue eyes twinkled. "Hop in!"

Puzzled, the boys climbed aboard. Sandy took off gracefully and soon they were soaring across Lake Carlopa.

"May I ask where we're going?" Tom said to Phyl with a grin.

"Carterton."

"What's there?"

Phyl smiled mischievously.

The answer became apparent when they reached their destination twenty minutes later. A carnival had been set up on the outskirts of Carterton, next to the town's tiny airfield.

"Yippee!" Bud burst out gleefully. "This is wonderful, Sandy! I haven't been to a carnival in a blue moon!"

As soon as they had landed and parked the plane, the four young people hurried off gaily on foot to the carnival grounds. A din of excitement filled the place.

The carnival was ablaze with color, highlighted by striped tents and clusters of toy balloons. Barkers shouted in front of the amusement concessions, while children shrieked and squealed with laughter on the fun rides and the merry-go-round.

"Oh, I'm so excited!" Phyl confessed. "Sandy, this is the best idea you ever had!"

"Check!" Tom agreed, laughing.

The two couples lunched on frankfurters and milk shakes, topped off with cones of pink cotton candy for the girls.

"Hey, let's show Sandy and Phyl what hot shots we are!" Bud proposed as they passed a shooting-gallery booth.

"Okay." Tom grinned. "But let's not run up the score on 'em too high!"

The girls selected guns and shot their round first. Bing! Bing! Bing! The traveling ducks went down faster than clay pigeons at a rifle match.

"Wow! Pretty good!" Bud gulped. Sandy and Phyl smiled innocently but said nothing.

When Tom and Bud's turn came, they were unable to beat the girls' high score. The boys looked at each other in deep chagrin as they laid down their guns.

Tom chuckled wryly. "You don't suppose this could have been a put-up job, too?" he quipped to Bud.

The girls burst out laughing. "Okay, we'll 'fess up!" Sandy giggled. "We've been taking shooting lessons from Chow!"

The boys vowed to do better at the next concession. This turned out to be a booth where the customers were pitching baseballs at a comical-looking dummy.

"Three shots for a quarter!" the barker shouted. "Nothin' to it, folks! Hit the dummy and down he goes! So step right up and win your little lady a prize!"

"Okay. Maybe our luck will turn here." Bud, who had been a fireball hurler on his high school team, grinned in anticipation.

As they waited their turn, a bystander snickered. "Hey, that dummy looks just like Longneck! Let's go tell him!"

Tom and Bud were amazed. Could the speaker be referring to Longneck Ebber?

Bud shot a quick glance at Tom. "Did you hear that?" he muttered.

"I sure did." Tom turned to the two girls. "Wait here, please. We'll be right back."

The man who had spoken, a burly, red-faced fellow, was already walking away with his companion. Tom and Bud followed them.

As they approached one of the carnival tents, Tom's heart gave a thump. Just ahead stood a tall, cadaverous man with a beaky nose—the same man shown in the FBI photos. He must be Longneck Ebber!

His eyes fell on the young inventor at almost the same instant that Tom recognized him. Ebber let out a yell of alarm to his two cronies.

"Run, you jugheads! That's Tom Swift right behind you!"

The red-faced man and his pal whirled in dismay, then took off like startled jack rabbits. Ebber was already plunging into the crowd. Tom and Bud dashed after the three men, but the fugitives scattered among the milling throng.

"Follow Ebber!" Tom cried out.

Ducking and weaving to avoid collisions with the carnival merrymakers, the two boys sprinted through the midway. But the crowds of people made it impossible to keep their quarry in sight. Tom and Bud soon gave up, realizing that Longneck Ebber could have slipped off in any of a dozen directions among the tents.

Disgusted by their bad luck, the boys rejoined Sandy and Phyl and told them what had happened. Tom spotted a policeman who was patrolling the carnival grounds. He gave the officer a full report,

Tom and Bud dashed after the fugitives

explaining that Ebber was wanted by the FBI.

"I'll phone headquarters right away and get a search started," the officer promised. "Those birds have probably gotten away by this time, but the State Police can set up roadblocks."

In spite of the unexpected incident, the young people thoroughly enjoyed their stay at the carnival. As dusk fell, they flew back to Shopton and finished the evening by attending an informal dance at the local country club.

That night and again on Sunday, Tom checked by telephone with the State Police. But his friend, Captain Rock, reported that they had found no trace of Longneck Ebber and his two cronies.

On Monday, at Enterprises, Tom was elated to hear from Art Wiltessa that the new de-organicizer was ready.

"Nice going, Art!" Tom congratulated the engineer. "Now for the city of gold!"

During the rest of the day and most of Tuesday, Tom made final arrangements for the expedition. Late that afternoon Lieutenant Brian Fraser arrived by jet plane from Washington. Fraser, a redhaired, pleasant-faced young Navy officer, had been assigned to replace Cromwell, who still had not recovered from the assault by Ebber and Judson. Tom noticed that the new man wore the twin gold dolphins of the submarine service.

"You'll be right in your element on this trip," he said as they shook hands.

Fraser grinned. "I'm looking forward to it!"

Tom explained that he planned to erect a permanent plastic dome over the undersea ruins, similar to the one that he had constructed at the Swifts' helium wells. Two cargo jetmarines would accompany the *Sea Hound* to set up the dome.

Early Wednesday morning Tom, Bud, Chow, Lieutenant Fraser, and Doc Simpson flew to Fearing Island, where the crews were standing by. Tom called an immediate conference to brief his men. Mel Flagler and Zimber Cox, two experienced pilots, had been chosen to command the cargo jetmarines.

Both craft were operated by hydraulic propulsion. They were large versions of Tom's original two-man model, used in his hunt for undersea pirates, and were specially adapted to cargo transport. Each had a round, oversized conning tower which also served as the loading hatch.

"Mel, your ship will carry the organ," Tom said, "and yours, Zimby, will carry the repelatron equipment. Keep your sonar- and hydrophones alert at all times, in case the Brungarians try to pitch us any curves."

"Aye-aye, skipper!" they acknowledged.

All three ships were ready for departure. Within an hour they submerged and streaked off through the waters of the Atlantic, with the *Sea Hound* in the lead.

"Some ship you have here!" Brian Fraser said

to Tom admiringly as they zoomed to a speed of eighty knots.

Bud grinned. "Wait'll you see her fly!"

The next morning they arrived at Tom's brilliantly lighted Helium City. The glistening plastic dome which housed the drill rigs, tanks, dormitory, and workshops, two miles under the ocean, made a thrilling spectacle. After a brief stop, the three submarines proceeded toward the undersea ruins.

So far, all had gone well, with no warning alerts from the sonar- or sound-detection equipment. Presently Tom flicked on his sonarphone mike to pass an order in code to Zimby Cox.

"Son to Sub Two. Come in, please!"

There was no response. Tom repeated his call without success, then signaled to Mel Flagler's craft.

"Right with you, skipper," Mel responded. "What's up?"

"I can't make contact," Tom explained. "Have you heard from Two?"

"Not since the last stop."

Thoroughly alarmed, Tom turned the *Sea Hound* around and made a quick sweep of the area. The cargo jetmarine which had failed to answer was nowhere within range of his powerful search beam or sonarscope!

CHAPTER VIII

FISH TALK

LIKE a mammoth eye, the *Sea Hound's* beam continued to probe the inky waters. Still its yellow glare did not reveal the missing Swift jetmarine.

Finally Tom ordered Mel Flagler's craft to join the search. Two hours went by as the sea-copter and jetmarine ranged over a wide area. At last Mel reported back soberly:

"No luck, skipper."

Tom's heart sank. The search seemed futile.

"Why not surface and use your radio?" Brian Fraser suggested. "Cox may be way off course."

"It's worth a try," Tom conceded. But unless the missing jetmarine had also surfaced, he knew there was little chance of an answer.

Shutting off the rotor, Tom sent the *Sea Hound* shooting upward at elevator speed. The waters outside the cabin window lightened first to gray, then to a rich bluish green as they approached the area penetrated by the sun's rays. Moments later, the sleek seacopter burst above the waves.

Tom pressed a button to raise the *Sea Hound's* antenna and switched on the radio.

"Sea Hound calling Swift Sub Two!" he called in code. "Can you read me, Zimby?" He repeated the question several times.

Still no response.

Finally giving up in despair, Tom beamed a long-range call over Enterprises' special frequency. Dilling, the Swifts' radio chief, answered. Tom asked if he had received any message from Cox's craft.

"Not a word, Tom. Anything wrong?"

"It's missing," the young inventor reported grimly.

After hearing the story, Dilling promised to direct all efforts toward contacting the lost cargo jetmarine or picking up word on its fate. Then he switched Tom over to Mr. Swift, in his private office.

"How goes it, son?" the scientist inquired.

When Tom broke the bad news, his father too became deeply worried. Were Zimby and his crew lying trapped, perhaps already dead, somewhere on the ocean bottom? Or had their craft been intercepted and captured by a Brungarian undersea raider?

"Could our State Department take any steps?" Tom asked, clutching at the only straw he figured was left.

"I'll ask our Embassy to press an official inquiry," Mr. Swift replied. "And I'll also request the Navy to organize a search. In the meantime, I'd advise you to go ahead with your project, Tom."

"All right, Dad. But I'll need a replacement for the repelatron gear aboard Zimby's sub."

Mr. Swift promised to dispatch another craft with the necessary equipment as fast as possible. Tom signed off after relaying an affectionate message to his family.

Once more the *Sea Hound* plunged to the ocean depths, where Tom made another attempt to contact Zimby's craft by sonarphone. No answer came and the group was heavyhearted over the mysterious fate of their lost comrades.

Bud, shaking himself out of the doldrums, finally said, "Tom, the ancient underwater layout will need a name, especially after you get things shined up for tourists. How about Aurum City?"

"Aurum City?" put in Chow, who had come forward to see if anyone was hungry. "Where in tarnation did you get that handle?"

"*Aurum* means 'gold,'" Bud explained. "One of the six words I remember from high school Latin," he added with a grin.

"Aurum City," the old Westerner repeated musingly, rolling the name over his tongue. "Hmm. Not bad, Buddy boy. I kind o' like it."

Tom agreed. "Aurum City it is."

Soon the jagged peaks of the Atlantic Ridge loomed through the murk. Tom decided to circle the area cautiously before setting up his work base. Slowing the rotors, so the *Sea Hound* would rise, he glided over the mountainous undersea formation and signaled Mel Flagler to follow.

Ten minutes later the sonarman suddenly sang out, "I've picked up something, skipper!"

"Where away?" Tom asked tensely.

"Approximately 030 degrees—range two miles and approaching fast! Can't make it out yet, but it looks like a sub!"

A wave of excitement and alarm enveloped the crew. Was the newcomer an enemy—a Brungarian raider? If so, the unarmed *Sea Hound* and Mel's craft might be in for some dangerous action!

"I sure am glad this lil ole seacopter's coated with Tomasite!" Chow muttered fervently.

"You can say that again!" Bud agreed. Tomasite, an amazing plastic, acted as a radiation shield and electromagnetic neutralizer. It also absorbed sonar "pings" and thus prevented the *Sea Hound* from showing up on an enemy scope.

Tom, meanwhile, grabbed the sonarphone mike to warn Mel Flagler.

"If that sub is the enemy's, won't they pick up your voice on their hydrophones?" Lieutenant Fraser asked, cool but frowning.

Tom grinned. "I won't talk in a human voice.

We have a special code for emergencies—a fish code. Listen!"

He proceeded to utter a series of strange sounds into the microphone—first a cowlike moo; then a rasping noise; finally, after a pause, several sharp staccato barks.

Fraser was baffled for a moment. But he quickly broke into a wide grin as he recognized the fish noises often picked up at sea: the whining call of a black angelfish, and the rasp of a spiny lobster, and the staccato barks of squirrelfish and grouper.

Tom listened intently for Mel's acknowledgment. To his amazement, a voice replied in plain English:

"Hi, you old fish! I'm back!"

"Zimby!" Tom was beside himself with joy. "You mean that's *you* we spotted on the scope?"

"In person, skipper!"

The crew burst into cheers as they realized the missing jetmarine had returned safely.

"But where the dickens did you disappear to?" Tom went on excitedly.

Cox replied that their sonarscope had detected a strange submarine, apparently dogging them. "So I figured I'd lead it on a wild-goose chase, in case it happened to be Brungarian," he explained.

Later, after shaking the craft off his trail, Zimby had heard Tom's calls but did not dare reply for fear of attracting the enemy again.

Tom chuckled in relief. "The whole United States Navy's looking for you guys!"

After ordering the two cargo jetmarines to proceed to Aurum City, Tom surfaced and radioed Enterprises. Both Dilling and Mr. Swift were delighted by the good news of Zimby's return.

"I'll notify Admiral Hopkins at once," Mr. Swift said. "And fortunately the extra sub is still loading and hasn't left yet."

Moments later, the *Sea Hound* was plunging back toward the Atlantic Ridge. Tom brought the seacopter to rest on a valley floor among the undersea peaks. The two cargo jetmarines were hovering nearby, their lights illumining the pillared ruins of the golden city.

"Incredible!" Lieutenant Fraser gasped, peering out in amazement at the scene. "What's the procedure now, Tom?"

"Bud and I will go over to Zimby's sub and start the repelatron working," Tom explained. "Take charge while I'm gone, Brian. And keep a sharp alert for enemy craft!"

The young inventor and Bud quickly climbed into Fat Man suits and propelled themselves toward Cox's cargo jetmarine. The boys entered through the air lock and crawled out of their steel eggs. Tom gave instructions.

"We'll need two men to help us set up the air machine, Zimby. In the meantime, please hoist the repelatron into the air lock."

"Right, skipper!"

Tom, Bud, and their two assistants, all clad in Fat Man suits, proceeded to set up the osmotic air conditioner on the outskirts of the city. This device would draw dissolved oxygen from the sea water to provide an atmosphere for the air bubble.

When they returned to the cargo jetmarine, the repelatron was standing ready for action in the air lock. It consisted of a large silvery sphere mounted on a metal platform, together with a console and electronic control panel. The sphere contained the radiator which beamed out repulsion waves in all directions.

Tom adjusted several tuning knobs, then gripped the repelatron control lever, ready to switch on power.

"Okay. Open the hatch, Bud!"

Bud twirled the powerful screw mechanism and the outer port of the air lock slid open. At the same moment, a balloon of air began to form in the water outside. Then the repelatron, still working, was hoisted out of the jetmarine and set onto the ocean floor. Its huge anchor sank into the ground.

"Thar she blows!" Bud grinned with excitement upon seeing the giant bubble of air that surrounded the whole jetmarine.

Steadily the repelling waves forced back the sea water on all sides. The bubble grew bigger and bigger until it took in both the *Sea Hound* and the other cargo jetmarine. Swelling still more, it spread over the whole area of the ruins.

When the bubble reached the point where the osmotic atmosphere conditioner was set up, Tom flicked the switch on a remote-control cable. Instantly the machine thrummed into action, spreading a pleasant, less humid atmosphere through the bubble. A green signal light flashed as normal air pressure was reached.

Tom opened his quartz view plate and climbed out of the Fat Man. "We're in business, fellows!" he announced, grinning.

Bud took off his undersea gear and followed Tom. Crewmen poured out of all three submarines, cheering. Within minutes, a number of Tom Sr.'s powerful searchlights had been set up, bathing the scene in daylike radiance.

"Welcome to Aurum City!" Bud yelled.

The pillared temples and once-magnificent buildings made a breath-taking sight, even though they were now encrusted with barnacles and other sea growths.

A thrill of awe swept over Tom. "Just think, Bud," he murmured, "we're probably the first humans to set foot in this city in thousands of years!"

"Gives me goose bumps!" Bud admitted.

Excitedly the two boys strolled up one of the ancient streets, now rank with slime and ocean vegetation. Stately columns lined the avenue on either side.

"I wonder what that was," Bud remarked. He pointed toward a splendid building, approached by wide stone steps leading up from the street. "City hall, maybe?"

Tom eyed the structure with keen interest. "Looks as though it might have been a palace," he commented.

As the boys turned off the avenue for a closer look, neither noticed that one of the columns had begun to sway. But a moment later, Tom, warned by some sixth sense, glanced back. His face blanched in horror.

"Look out, Bud!" he shrieked.

The column was toppling straight toward them!

CHAPTER IX

A DANGEROUS LEAK

TOM grabbed Bud's arm and yanked him out of
the way in the nick of time. The palace column
landed with a rumbling crash, missing the boys by
a fraction of an inch.

"Good grief!" Bud murmured as he steadied
himself on legs that were shaky with fright. "Man,
I could feel the breeze as that went by!" he gasped.

Tom grinned weakly and agreed. "If the column
had beamed us, pal, we'd be flatter than pancakes
by now!"

A voice made the boys turn their heads. "Are
you all right?" Lieutenant Fraser cried out, run-
ning up anxiously.

Tom and Bud nodded, still a bit breathless.
"Pulse rate slightly abnormal but otherwise
okay," Tom quipped. "Let's hope no other columns or buildings around here start getting
wobbly!"

Brian, spellbound by the wonders of Aurum City, could only shake his head in awe. "Tom, it's a wonder *any* of this is still standing!" he said. "Imagine! A city that's been lost for untold centuries beneath the sea! And here we are, walking its streets!"

"This may be one of the greatest archaeological finds in history," Bud remarked.

"But where did it come from? I mean—what civilization *was* this?" the lieutenant asked.

"We think it *may* be the lost Atlantis," Tom replied, "but I'm hoping this expedition may turn up some clues that will give us the answer." He went on to explain the legend deciphered by the two government oceanographers who had first helped him locate the sunken city.

These two men had discovered an ancient Peruvian inscription about the original Incas of South America. It told how they had come over the sea from a far-off land which had been engulfed by a terrible earthquake and flood.

"The data given in the inscription pointed to this very spot," Tom ended. "It was also near some peaks shaped like man-made pyramids which I had already spotted in the Atlantic Ridge. But it'll take a lot of work yet, Brian, to piece together an accurate explanation."

The two boys and the red-haired Navy officer strolled back toward the *Sea Hound,* their shoes slipping and squelching in the ooze that covered the ancient street. Bud noticed that Tom seemed plunged in deep thought.

"What's going on in that supersonic brain of yours, genius boy?" he asked with a grin.

"A scientific puzzler, Bud," the young inventor replied. "Have you two noticed the absence of sea life on the floor of this city? Of course there's plenty of undersea vegetation," he added, "but no *animal* forms of marine life."

"That's so," Brian Fraser agreed. "But aren't your repelatron force waves pushing out the fish and other sea creatures?"

Tom shook his head. "No, the machine's tuned only to repel sea water. It would have no more effect on fish than it does on us."

"What's the answer then, Professor?" Bud asked.

Tom shrugged. "I can only guess. But maybe there's something here in Aurum City which is poisonous or obnoxious to animal life."

"Meaning us?" Bud asked.

"Not necessarily. Relax, pal!" Tom grinned and patted his friend's arm. "It may be simply that these buildings are giving off a radiation of low intensity."

"What type of radiation?" Brian asked.

"Some form that's invisible to human eyes," Tom replied, "and as harmless to us as sunlight, yet repulsive to marine animals."

"Interesting theory," Brian conceded. "Can you test it?"

Tom mulled over the problem. "Let's try turning off the lights," he suggested. "If there *is* any radiation present, it may show up as a faint luminescence."

Bud passed the word among the crewmen and Tom walked over to the solar-battery switch box controlling the searchlights. He opened the switch. Instantly the undersea city was plunged into total darkness.

"No glow so far as I can see," Lieutenant Fraser remarked.

Tom sighed. "We can scratch *that* theory, I guess."

At that moment a yell came from Chow. "Hey! What in tarnation's splashin' me?"

Hastily Tom flicked on the switch and Aurum City was again bathed in brilliance. Cries of alarm rose from the crewmen as they saw water pouring into the bubble!

"Brand my periscope, we've sprung a leak!" Chow hollered. The ranch cook, already half drenched, galloped clear of the torrent.

The air space would soon be flooded, with disastrous results to the occupants!

"All hands back aboard!" Tom shouted.

He dashed toward the repelatron. To his amazement, the machine was unmanned!

"We've sprung a leak!" Chow shouted

Quickly Tom's eyes scanned the control dials. The selector needle had strayed almost two points off peak tuning. Tom's lean, sinewy hands flew over the control panel, adjusting various knobs. Gradually the needle flickered back to correct position.

"Hooray! The leak's stopped!" Chow shouted.

As Tom mopped his brow in relief, a voice spoke behind him. It was Mack Avery, the technician assigned to watch the repelatron.

"My fault, skipper," he confessed shamefacedly. "The needle was holding steady, so I figured it would be all right if I wandered off to see the sights for a while. Boy, was I wrong!"

Tom nodded understandingly. "Okay, Mack. But don't let it happen again."

In spite of his calm manner, the young inventor was upset by the brief emergency. What if another mishap occurred with the repelatron, trapping his men before they could reach safety? Tom shuddered at the horrible picture that rose to mind— men being crushed by the pressure of two-mile-deep ocean water! To discuss the problem, Tom called a conference with his two jetmarine captains and Lieutenant Fraser.

"Why not double the watch on the repelatron?" Mel Flagler proposed. "Then if one man goofs off, there'd still be someone tending the controls."

"That would be a lot safer, of course," Tom

agreed. "But what if the machine itself conks out? Would we have time to repair it?"

"Then how about ordering your men to keep emergency diving rigs handy at all times?" Brian Fraser suggested.

Tom pointed out that there were not enough Fat Man suits for everyone. And the other deep-sea outfits carried aboard were undependable at such tremendous depth and pressure.

In the end, Tom decided to radio Shopton to send the other repelatron by jetmarine. With an extra machine on stand-by at all times, the danger of a disaster would be eliminated.

"Keep your men close to the ships while I surface," Tom told Mel and Zimby.

"Aye-aye, skipper!"

Boarding the *Sea Hound* with Bud, Brian Fraser, and his crew, Tom zoomed toward the surface. At a depth of about a thousand feet came a cry from the sonarman:

"Sub approaching, skipper! Bearing 250!"

Quick as a flash, Tom gunned the throttle and shoved the control wheel forward. The *Sea Hound* plummeted downward.

Safe from detection with its Tomasite coating, the Swift craft hovered at a mile depth until the sonar showed that the mysterious submarine had passed out of range.

"Let's chase it!" Bud said eagerly. "If it's Brungarian, we may learn what they're up to!"

But Tom shook his head cautioningly. "Not worth taking a chance, Bud. It's more important to keep our own presence a secret."

Surfacing, Tom switched on the radio and cut in the automatic scrambler. With this device operating, an enemy would hear only garbled static even if he monitored their signal.

Within seconds, Tom's call brought a response from Enterprises. Dilling turned him over to Mr. Swift. When Tom explained the situation, his father promised to dispatch the extra repelatron at once.

"By the way, son," the scientist added gravely, "I've just had some news from the State Department."

"Bad news, Dad?" Tom asked, detecting the somber note in his father's voice.

"I'm afraid it may prove so. According to our American intelligence agents, a group of Brungarian scientists are working secretly with some unknown foreigners."

Mr. Swift hesitated a moment, then went on, "Their aim has not yet been uncovered, Tom, but it seems to concern the sunken city!"

CHAPTER X

POISON GAS

TOM'S blue eyes kindled with alarm. "Dad, that would explain the sub that trailed Zimby! Incidentally, I think we spotted it again!" He reported the mysterious craft which had passed over the *Sea Hound*.

"I'll notify Central Intelligence and send you any later word when the repelatron comes down," Mr. Swift promised.

After signing off, Tom gunned the rotor and the *Sea Hound* submerged. As they plunged toward the bottom, he discussed the intelligence report with Bud and Lieutenant Fraser.

"I'll bet my last nickel those 'unknown foreigners' include Longneck Ebber," Bud snorted.

"No takers, Bud." Tom grinned wryly. "I'm already convinced that Ebber and Judson were hired by our Brungarian enemies."

"If you're right, Tom," mused Brian, "the Brungarians may not stop at just sabotage and spying." The young Navy officer's face looked grim.

"You mean they might even attack our setup at Aurum City?" Bud asked, wide-eyed.

"The Brungarian Navy might move in," Brian pointed out.

"You may have a point there," Tom conceded. "We'd better keep a sharp alert at all times."

As they zoomed down through the pitch-dark waters, the glow from Aurum City came into view. During their absence, a hard, shimmering plastic dome had been erected over the working area. Tom parked the *Sea Hound* between this and the outer rim of the air bubble. Then he and his crew entered the dome through the zippered flap.

"Looks as though you fellows have been busy while we were gone," Tom said with a congratulatory smile to Mel Flagler and Zimby Cox.

"We also hooked up the purifying equipment to the air conditioner," Zimby said.

"Good work!" Tom gave them each a hearty slap on the back. "Then we may as well go ahead with our job of cleaning off these gold buildings."

The de-organic-izer was unloaded from Flagler's jetmarine and quickly assembled. Tom stepped aboard the cab to make a final instrument check before the device was wheeled into action.

"Hey, boss!" Tom looked up and saw Chow's bald head poking into the cab. "Kin I come aboard, too, an' see how she works?"

"Sure, if you can squeeze in, old-timer!"

Beaming, Chow hoisted his rotund bulk up onto the operator's platform. His eyes bulged admiringly as he watched Tom's fingers move about the control board, adjusting various dials.

"Brand my biscuits, boss," Chow murmured, "you kin play this lil ole contraption like it was a pipe organ!"

Tom grinned without speaking. But the onlookers picked up the leathery Texan's remark and began needling him jokingly.

As the cook blushed, Bud followed up with an off-key rendition of "When the Organ Played at Twilight."

Brian grinned and remarked, "Tom, I think your invention has just been officially nicknamed."

Tom chuckled. "Suits me, Brian. Just as long as it makes sweet music when I try it out!"

With his checkout completed, Tom started the traction motor. The organ rolled forward on its caterpillar treads until Tom brought it to rest, facing a group of statues. They stood in a row before a lofty porticoed building.

"Suppose we see what these statues look like underneath all that gunk," Tom said.

Switching on the infrared unit, he moved a lever which started the localator vacuum producer. He aimed the intake at the nearest statue and instantly it began to whisk off the slimy coating.

"Like a giant razor in action," Bud remarked.

Tom grinned, as he fingered the S-Co controls which changed the molecules of the organic waste into easily stored compounds.

The watchers gasped as the slimy statue was gradually transformed into a glittering gold animal god! The human face had a hawk's beak and folded wings on a catlike body. As Tom proceeded, other statues turned out to be crouching lions or jaguars with men's features. One depicted a huge serpent coiled around a goddess.

"They're solid gold!" Fraser gasped.

"They may have just a golden shell over some other material," Tom said cautiously, after getting out of the cab to examine the statues more closely.

"What type of people could have made them, skipper?" Doc Simpson put in with keen scientific curiosity.

"They look something like those Mayan statues we saw in Yucatan, don't they?" Bud said.

Tom nodded thoughtfully. "Their form is similar. But I'd say their faces are more like a mixture of the Oriental and South Sea sculptures on display in our Shopton Museum."

Continuing with the cleanup process, Tom uncovered the front wall of the building. Its majestic outlines, gleaming with gold, brought awed murmurs from the crewmen.

"Must have been a temple," Doc commented.

"Probably," Tom agreed. "But its architecture is different from anything I've ever seen pictured."

Deciding that it might be well to check on the repelatron, Tom turned the organ over to Bud and hurried back to look.

"Any trouble?" he asked the two men on watch.

They shook their heads. "She's ticking like a watch, skipper," one replied.

Tom scanned the dials to make sure. Then he glanced back at the work being done. To his amazement, the men were behaving strangely. They were moving in slow, jerky fashion and clutching their throats.

"Good night!" Tom gasped. "What's going on?"

He ran toward the group. Almost instantly, his nostrils caught a whiff of a flowerlike odor.

"Flowers?" Tom halted, puzzled, trying to identify the odor.

Then his face went pale as the answer clicked in his mind. *Cyanogen gas!* The deadly vapor could wipe out every person in Aurum City within minutes!

"Bud!" Tom yelled. "Turn off the organ!"

Like a flash, he himself darted toward the air machine and purifying equipment and speeded up both machines. Their droning hum rose to a high-pitched whine. Without pausing, Tom circled the temple on a dead run, shepherding everyone to safety.

"All hands, back to the submarines!" he shouted.

As soon as all were aboard, Tom ordered an immediate muster on the three submarines. Mel Flagler reported that his entire outfit was accounted for. But the senior crewman on Cargo Sub Two replied that Zimby Cox was missing.

"We have Zimby here in the *Sea Hound*," Tom radioed back. "Take charge, Mike, till I sound the all clear."

Presently Doc Simpson came to report on the victims. "They're okay," he informed Tom. "Zimby and Fraser were in bad shape, but I've given them oxygen and a stimulant. They should be back on their feet soon with no ill effects."

Tom, sweating with anxiety and exertion, wiped his arm across his brow. "Whew!" he muttered thankfully. "That was a close call, Doc!"

Doc nodded. "Tom, where did that cyanogen come from?"

"I don't know for sure yet," Tom admitted. "But I have a hunch it may have been formed by the action of the organ."

As soon as the atmosphere was purified, Tom checked the device. His suspicions seemed to be borne out after careful testing.

"The S-Co was releasing carbon and nitrogen too fast," Tom explained to Bud. "They combined to form the cyanogen gas."

"Any way to fix it?" Bud asked.

Tom shrugged and ran his fingers through his hair, while his forehead puckered in a worried frown. "For the moment I'm stumped, pal. But I'd better come up with an answer fast, or our whole project here will be stopped cold!"

Returning to the *Sea Hound,* Tom worked on the problem steadily for several hours, not even pausing for the evening meal. At midnight Bud and Doc Simpson found him slumped over his desk in his tiny laboratory compartment.

"Poor guy! He's passed out from sheer exhaustion," Doc commented.

"Come on! Let's put him to bed," Bud said.

When Tom awoke in his bunk the next morning, his brain held a clear answer to his problem. "I'll simply alter the storage system so that the hydrogen and nitrogen from the organic waste can be combined to form fuel gas," he told himself. "The carbon can be combined with oxygen to form carbon dioxide and pumped off into the ocean!"

Elated by the simple solution, Tom leaped from his bunk and began to dress.

"Hi, Doc!" he exclaimed with a grin a moment later as the medic walked into the compartment. "Guess I conked out last night, but I feel fine!"

"That's good. You'll need to be in sound shape to take the news I have," Doc Simpson replied. "The sub bringing the extra repelatron has just arrived. We found a mysterious stowaway aboard!"

CHAPTER XI

STOWAWAY PRISONER

"A STOWAWAY?"

The news took Tom by surprise. He stared at
Doc Simpson in alarm. A flurry of questions rose
to Tom's lips, but he realized that it would be
simpler to find out the answers himself.

"I'll talk to him!" the young inventor flung
the words over his shoulder as he rushed out of
the compartment.

Doc followed and they ran toward the newly
arrived jetmarine which was berthed nearby. Tom
entered through the air lock and scrambled down
the ladder. Inside the cargo hold, he found Bud
and another crewman gripping the prisoner.

"We found this guy hiding down here!" Bud
snapped angrily.

Longneck Ebber!

Tom, his jaw set grimly, gave the stowaway a
penetrating stare. "All right, Ebber. Talk!"

Ebber's face was sullen, and for several moments he remained silent. He shifted his eyes uneasily under Tom's steely gaze. Finally he spoke.

"No sense gettin' sore, Swift," he whined. "I know I got no business bein' here, but can't we make a deal? Look—you guys turn me loose an' I'll talk plenty! I can tell you lots o' things you want to know! How about it?"

"Make a deal—with somebody like you?" The young inventor's blue eyes glinted fire. "We're at the bottom of the ocean, Ebber, and you're our prisoner. We don't have to make bargains!"

Ebber went sickly white. He glanced from one person to another as if looking for a sympathetic face. He found none.

"Wh-wh-what do you mean, Swift?" the prisoner quavered finally. "Now listen here! You guys can't get away with pullin' any rough stuff!"

Tom's lips tightened. "Did you think of that when you and Judson beat up that Navy officer?"

Ebber was trembling like a leaf now. "Y-y-you can't bluff me!" he shrilled. "You guys wouldn't dare hurt me! I got my rights. . . ."

His voice cracked and died away as he saw Brian Fraser and several husky crewmen edging closer. Their fists were clenched menacingly.

Suddenly Ebber's legs gave way. He sank down on a crate of supplies and mopped his brow.

"Okay," he mumbled. "I'll talk. What do you want to know?"

"Everything," Tom snapped grimly. "You can start by telling us how you got aboard."

Ebber hesitated a moment, then said, "I—er—stopped a skinny fella like me on his way to work at Enterprises an' took his pass an' bracelet, so I got in easy. Then I waited for a chance to shut myself into one o' the crates, goin' to be shipped down here." He added ruefully, "I should 'a' stayed in it an' you wouldn't 'a' caught me."

Tom frowned angrily. "Who was the man you attacked?"

"Sam Green. Oh, I didn't hurt him."

"We'll find out about that. If he wasn't in condition to report the attack so you could be caught, he must have been in bad shape," Tom retorted. Then he asked, "Longneck, who hired you and Judson?"

"It was some foreign bunch," Ebber confessed. "At least, I guess they're foreigners. Their agent got in touch with us. He's the only guy we actually talked to."

"What were your instructions?" Tom asked.

Ebber flushed nervously. "Well, Judson used to be a plane mechanic before he went in for fancy bookkeepin'," the stowaway explained. "Joe's a smart cookie around machinery, so he was to handle the sabotage end of it. Between us, we were supposed to try an' keep you from making any underwater trips."

Tom's gaze bored into the prisoner. "Your pals

didn't make a very successful trip themselves. We found their remains!"

Tom was hoping that Ebber might be startled into revealing some clue to the sunken hulk. Instead, Ebber was frightened speechless! The muscles in his scrawny neck twitched as he gulped fearfully.

"Listen! I don't want no part o' this undersea bone yard!" he gasped when he found his voice. "Please! Send me back! I don't even care if you turn me over to the FBI!"

Bud winked at Tom as if to say, "You will!"

Tom went on, "Longneck, you're staying right here. And if you don't work and follow orders, you won't be called when rations are handed out. Understand?"

Tom paused to let his words sink in, then went on, "What's the name of this foreign agent who contacted you?"

"I don't know his real name," Longneck replied. "Just his nickname—it's Decko."

"Maybe we could jog your memory!" Lieutenant Fraser growled.

Ebber cringed as the red-haired Navy officer loomed over him. "It's the truth!" Longneck whined. "I don't even know where the guy hangs out. The first time we met him was in some waterfront dive. After that, it was always some different place. He'd call us beforehand to tell us where."

"What did he look like?" Bud put in.

"Well . . . let's see." Ebber scowled in concentration and rubbed his sweating palms together as he tried to recall Decko's appearance. "He's short, heavy-set, an' has a big jaw an' a bullet-shaped head."

"What color hair?" Bud prodded.

"Black, cut real close. He wears horn-rimmed glasses, too, an' always has on dark clothes."

Bud glanced at Tom warily. Was Longneck Ebber trying to mislead them? Tom decided to check.

"Wait a minute!" the young inventor exclaimed, snapping his fingers. "I know Decko! But he sure doesn't look the way you described him, Longneck! He's blond and fairly tall. And he likes flashy clothes!"

Longneck looked puzzled. "Not the guy I'm talkin' about," he insisted. "He's dark an' short!"

Tom, watching Ebber's expression closely, decided that he was telling the truth.

"Okay, maybe you're on the level," he conceded. "I guess it's another Decko I know."

Tom now called to two crewmen, Strong and Ehler, and assigned them the job of guarding the prisoner around the clock.

"Where should we keep him, skipper?" Strong asked. "Down here in the hold?"

Tom shook his head. "No, let him earn his keep. Put him with the regular work crews. But keep an eye on him every minute!"

Strong and Ehler grinned and saluted. "Roger!"

Tom ordered Mel Flagler to surface and radio a full report on the stowaway to Dilling. Meanwhile, after a hearty breakfast of Chow's griddle-cakes, Tom threw himself into the job of cleaning up Aurum City.

The organ continued to work like a charm. As it stripped away the slime and muck, without removing any of the gold beneath, Bud slapped Tom on the back.

"Genius boy, that's one of the most marvelous precision instruments I've ever seen."

Tom grinned. "It's working pretty well so far," he admitted. "But too slow, pal. Don't forget, I

promised to help Dad locate the rare metals. I must get along faster with this job. You take over here while I see what I can dream up."

The young inventor stood lost in thought for nearly ten minutes. Then he went to his laboratory on the *Sea Hound* and worked for hours on a nucleonic accelerator. Satisfied, he and other engineers fitted it into the de-organic-izer. The cleaning process was stepped up double! Buildings and statues began to emerge in their original golden glory. By noon of the next day a whole street of Aurum City had been restored to its onetime splendor.

"Boy, this is like living in the middle of Fort Knox!" Bud joked at lunch.

"Brand my prospector's belt!" Chow called out. "I'm sure goin' to count all them gold statues an' columns afore we leave here!" The ex-ranch cook was hustling up and down the mess compartment in his undershirt, dishing out steaming bowls of Texas chili.

Suddenly there was a half-stifled scream from Brian Fraser. He sprang up from the table amid a clatter of dishes.

"I'm burning up!" the officer yelled.

As his messmates looked on in horror, Brian ripped off his shirt and began scratching frantically. His face, arms, and neck turned flaming red. Tom and others rushed to his assistance.

"Good night, Brian!" Tom cried. "What's wrong?"

"I . . . I . . . don't know!" Fraser gasped.

The rash was rapidly spreading over his chest and body. His eyes were bulging. The officer twisted and writhed in agony.

Tom shouted an order. "Quick, Bud! Radio for Doc Simpson! He's in Sub Two. Bring him here on the run!"

CHAPTER XII

DEADLY FUNGUS

DOC arrived within moments, clutching a medical kit. His eyes were grim as he examined the scarlet splotches on Brian Fraser's skin. Pulling out a bottle of antihistamine tablets, he shook out three.

"Here! Take these!"

Brian gulped them down with difficulty. He was trying hard to control himself, but again and again the burning rash threw him into fresh spasms of agony.

"Easy now! This should help!" Doc muttered. He hastily shook a bottle of cream-colored lotion and plucked a wad of cotton from the kit.

Moistening the cotton, he smeared the lotion over the inflamed areas. Brian shuddered and gasped as he tried to hold still for treatment.

"Doing any good?" asked Bob Jeffers, one of the crewmen. He and his mates had left the mess table to watch anxiously.

The answer soon became frighteningly apparent. New splotches of rash were appearing. Even worse, Brian was having difficulty in breathing.

"Brand my cactus salad, the poor maverick's strangulatin'!" Chow cried.

Doc grabbed Brian's wrist and felt for his pulse. It was slowing dangerously.

"Quick! Hold his arm!" the medic told Tom. As Tom did so, Doc scrubbed a patch of skin with alcohol and plunged in a hypodermic needle. "It's a heart stimulant," he explained tersely.

The injection seemed to give Brian new strength. His breathing eased somewhat and his pulse became stronger. Doc left the compartment for a moment and Tom hurried after him.

"Any idea what's causing it?" the young inventor asked fearfully.

Doc Simpson shook his head. His face was etched with lines of worry. "Frankly, Tom, I've never seen or heard of anything like it," he confessed. "I'm hoping to find some clue in my reference text on skin diseases."

The young medic rummaged through his locker and pulled out a thick volume. He was just thumbing through it when a yell of pain rang from the adjoining compartment.

"That's Bud!" Tom cried, turning pale.

Doc Simpson flung down his book and dashed after Tom. Their fears were realized as they saw Bud clawing off his T shirt. His face and neck were mottled with crimson splotches.

"Please! Do something, Doc!" Bud gasped. "I'm on fire!"

"Take it easy, pal!" Tom pleaded. "Scratching will only make it worse!"

Doc hastily dosed Bud with antihistamine and began swabbing him with lotion. He was only half finished when Chow and two other crewmen began breaking out with the same fiery rash.

"Great snakes!" the cook spluttered. "This is worse 'n a hideful o' buckshot an' cayenne pepper!"

Fear spread through the onlookers like a fever at sight of the terrifying symptoms. Tom rallied the crew into action before anyone could voice his panicky thoughts.

"Come on! Lend a hand, you fellows!" he snapped. "Doc needs help in treating these men!"

The crew responded willingly. Stripping off the victims' clothes, they took over the job of swabbing on the lotion. Doc, meanwhile, doled out antihistamine pills and gave hypodermic injections to the sufferers with cool efficiency.

"Could it be food poisoning?" Tom asked, as he sterilized one man's arm before Doc Simpson jabbed in the needle.

The medic shook his head. "Out of the question, I should say. But they might be allergic to something in the atmosphere around here. I'm trying antihistamines."

Fortunately, Brian was no worse. Though the

rash still itched agonizingly, it had ceased to spread.

But new trouble was in store. As Doc finished injecting the victims, Zimby Cox came rushing aboard. He stopped in dismay at sight of the red-splotched sufferers.

"Good night! So they've got it, too!"

"Somebody else?" Tom asked.

Zimby nodded breathlessly. "Two men on watch aboard my sub and one of Mel's crew."

"Get 'em over here fast!" Tom ordered. "Doc will have to treat them all together!"

The mess gear was hastily cleared away, so the compartment could be turned into a makeshift sick bay. Tom fought down a wave of despair, but his brain was working coolly. He pondered Doc's remark about the possibility of an allergy caused by some irritant in the atmosphere.

Then another thought clicked in Tom's mind. He recalled having noticed how animal life had never come to feed on the organic matter covering Aurum City. Was this due to the same cause?

"Maybe the answer lies in the undersea vegetation growing on the buildings!" Tom reasoned. "Nearly everybody's touched it and some of us may be more sensitive to the stuff than others!"

He voiced his hunch to Doc Simpson. "Do you suppose this rash is caused by some kind of fungus which grows down here?" Tom asked. "Would that explain the symptoms?"

Doc paused in his work. "It might," he agreed, frowning thoughtfully. "The rash has certain fungus characteristics—like athlete's foot, for instance. You know how that can burn."

He added in a discouraged voice, "But even if you're right, Tom, it's not much help. None of the medication I've tried seems to be having much effect."

Tom gripped the medic's arm. "Then let's try something else, Doc," he murmured. "I have a wild idea, but it might just work. Get Brian outside and I'll treat him first!"

Doc stared after the young inventor. His surprise changed to bewilderment when he glanced out the cabin window a few minutes later.

The spectromarine selector was rolling up to the *Sea Hound* on its tractor treads! Tom waved from the cab.

"Good night! What's he intending to do?" Zimby muttered, as puzzled as everyone else.

"I don't know," Doc Simpson replied, "but whatever he's up to, Tom usually has a good reason for it. Help me get Brian out there!"

Between them, Doc and Zimby assisted the almost frantic officer out through the air lock.

"This may be risky," Tom warned Brian, "but if it's a fungus that's causing your rash, I believe the organ may be able to remove it. Are you game to try?"

"I'll—I'll try anything!" Fraser gasped.

Without another word, Tom aimed the intake at Fraser's chest. A faint, purring hum was heard as Tom flicked on low power and manipulated the controls.

"It's working!" Zimby cried moments later. Doc's face brightened into a joyful smile.

The ugly scarlet patches were vanishing from Brian's skin! Within a few minutes the poison fungus had been completely removed!

As Doc signaled the good news, Tom shut off power and leaped from the cab. "How do you feel, Brian?" he asked.

The Navy officer was dazed with relief. "It's a miracle, Tom! The burning is gone!"

Tom and Zimby watched eagerly as Doc examined the patient. Other members of the crew stood by or peered from the *Sea Hound's* window.

Only faintly reddened areas remained to show where Brian had suffered the fungus attack. Doc straightened up, grinning, and pumped Tom's arm in a hearty handshake.

"Skipper, you've done it!" he reported. "The fastest skin cure on record! That machine of yours has just made medical history!"

Cheers burst from the crewmen's throats.

Tom smiled but wasted no time on acknowledging the congratulations from all sides. Bud, Chow, and the other victims were still in urgent need of treatment. One by one, they took their turns under the purring snout of the de-organic-izer. In every case, the burning fungus was stripped away as if by magic.

"Brand my hide, boss," Chow exulted, trembling with relief, "you're the rip-snortin'est Injun medicine man I ever did see!"

Tom grinned and tried to hide his own emotion. "I had to do something, Chow. Without the best lil ole range cook this side of Texas, our whole expedition would've been plumb ruined!"

"And don't forget the best copilot this side of Mars!" Bud quipped, gripping his pal's hand. "What Chow said goes double for me, Tom!"

As a final touch, Doc Simpson applied a cooling ointment to the afflicted men. Two hours later all were well. Tom ordered that hereafter special salve and gloves be used by everyone while working in Aurum City. Later, while he was in his tiny laboratory compartment at work with the spectroscope, Bud and Brian entered.

"What cooks, Doctor Swift?" Bud asked. "Hatching some new medical miracles?"

Tom grinned, then turned serious. "I've just been analyzing a specimen of the fungus growth on the gold surface of these undersea buildings."

"Can you identify it?" Brian Fraser asked.

Tom shook his head. "So far as I know, it doesn't occur on land. However, I've found out one interesting thing—it contains thorium."

"Thorium!" Bud whistled in surprise. "Hey, that stuff is radioactive, isn't it?"

"It sure is." Tom scowled and rubbed his jaw thoughtfully. "Of course we're dealing here with tiny amounts in the form of organic compounds. Which is pretty unusual, by the way, because thorium doesn't ordinarily enter into the make-up of living cells. That probably explains why deep-sea animal life avoids Aurum City."

The conversation broke off as Chow stumped into the compartment. The usually good-natured chef wore a grumpy look.

"Something wrong, old-timer?" Tom asked.

"Aw, it's that polecat, Longneck Ebber," Chow grumbled.

"What's he been up to?" Bud put in.

"Nothin'! That's jest it!" Chow retorted. "He don't do a lick o' work. He eats like a hoss, an' when it comes to eavesdroppin' that galoot's got ears longer'n a tired mule."

Tom frowned. "He's a problem, all right, Chow, but if we send him back to the States, he might have a chance to talk and spill the news about Aurum City. I hate to risk it."

Chow shook his head darkly. "Wal, mebbe so. But that coyote Longneck spells trouble, boss!"

CHAPTER XIII

AN INKY EXPLOSION

BUD and Brian Fraser looked worried.

"Chow may have a point there, Tom," Bud said. "I don't trust that creep Ebber myself. Having him around is like taking chances with a time bomb. It could go off in our faces!"

Fraser agreed. "Another thing. If you keep Longneck under cover here, isn't it possible that his Brungarian pals may come hunting for him?"

Tom mulled over this unpleasant dilemma. "You may be right," he conceded, "although I sure can't see the Brungarians losing any sleep over Longneck's fate. Just the same, I'd better check with Dad. I'll ask him to talk the matter over with the FBI."

The young inventor went on to say that he thought the United States should publicly claim Aurum City, and take official steps to guard it from marauders. Mr. Swift could propose this to the State and Defense departments.

"But first," Tom added, "I'd like to survey this whole undersea site and make sure how far it extends. That'll give our government an exact basis for staking its claim."

The next morning, the crew of the *Sea Hound* took their stations aboard the craft. Tom threw a lever extending its caterpillar treads and drove the seacopter into the water beyond the air bubble.

As he gunned the rotor and steering jets, the sleek craft took off like a darting fish. Soaring above the plastic dome, they glided through the dark waters.

"Switch on our searchlight, Bud," Tom directed.

An instant later the yellow beam cut a brilliant slash through the darkness. The rugged peaks of the Atlantic Ridge formation stood out on either side.

"Bud says there's a religious ceremonial ground somewhere near here," Brian said.

"That's right," Tom replied. "I'm heading for the spot. We'll see the pyramids I told you about."

Aurum City had been built in a canyon enclosed by beetling rock walls. These parted into a great valley beyond the city's outskirts.

The *Sea Hound's* beam swept the valley floor as they glided along. Here and there stood crumbling stone huts, overgrown with seaweed and ocean vegetation.

"Wonder who lived here?" Brian mused.

"Probably these were peasant apartment houses," Tom deduced. "In fact, this whole area may once have been a green, verdant valley with flocks of livestock and cultivated fields."

Aurum, he conjectured, was no doubt the capital city of this lost civilization.

"Just think," Tom went on. "An unknown people settled this valley thousands of years ago. They grew skilled enough in art and architecture to build splendid gold palaces and temples. They must have had good farmers, too, to feed the population. Then one day disaster struck—a flood wiping out the work of centuries. And the whole land sank under the ocean!"

Bud and Lieutenant Fraser stared out at the barren scene, awed by the picture Tom's words had painted.

"Let's hope no such disaster ever happens to *our* civilization," Brian muttered.

"I'm sure it won't," Tom said firmly. "Dad feels, and so do I, that mankind can build a wonderful future with the discoveries of science."

As the valley widened into an open plain, the *Sea Hound* roved back and forth, exploring for further signs of human habitation. Tom took navigational fixes at a number of points and sketched out a rough map of the area.

Presently another spur of the Atlantic Ridge rose ahead. Curiously pointed peaks loomed into view.

"Here are the pyramids," Tom said.

"Good night!" Brian murmured half-jokingly. "It's like seeing Egypt under water!"

The huge monuments appeared to have been carved from solid rock. They were grouped in a circle under the shadow of a towering undersea mountain.

Tom nosed the *Sea Hound* deftly in among the pyramids. At the center of the formation stood a flat altar, built from slabs of rock.

"Oh—oh!" Bud shuddered. "I wonder if they used that altar for sacrifices to their gods?"

"Very likely," Tom agreed. "But not necessarily human sacrifices, so let's not get gruesome, pal!" He added, "Well, let's go back. I think we've seen about all there is."

Tom slowed the rotor and eased back on the control wheel. The *Sea Hound* rose sharply, giving those aboard a wider, more panoramic view of the scene below. Leveling off, Tom sent the sea-copter spearing back toward Aurum City.

Bud was thoughtful. "Remember those carvings we spotted on one pyramid during our last trip here?" he remarked to Tom presently.

Tom nodded. "They were pretty well faded and covered over with sea growth. But I'd sure like to know what they mean!"

"Same here!"

Tom fell silent a moment, then went on, "You know, Bud, it's strange that we haven't found other carvings right in Aurum City. Almost every civilization leaves some kind of markings on its public buildings."

Bud's eyes kindled with interest. "Wow! You mean those carvings on the pyramid may have been made by someone else?"

"Just a hunch." Tom smiled. "You're probably thinking the same thing I am. Those carvings did look a bit like space symbols!"

"Space symbols?" Lieutenant Fraser looked puzzled. "What do you mean?"

Tom related how a strange black missile from outer space had plunged to earth at Swift Enterprises months before. The missile was covered with queer mathematical symbols. Tom and his father had succeeded in translating the markings, apparently made by beings from another planet.

Later, the Swifts had made contact with these beings, using the same code. Messages were beamed by a powerful radio transmitter and picked up on an oscilloscope type of receiver. It was their space friends who had moved the phantom satellite, Nestria, into orbit about the earth. They had also aided Tom on his later voyages to the moon.

"But how in the world could such creatures have made markings on those pyramids, even before they sank under the ocean?" Brian asked.

"We know they made at least one voyage to Earth centuries ago," Tom replied. "We found their symbols carved on some Mayan ruins in Mexico, telling how their spaceship had crashed. They might have left marks on these Aurum pyramids on some earlier voyage."

Tom added that he hoped to bring his electronic retroscope to Aurum City some time later and try to bring the faded carving into sharper focus.

After a final survey of the outlying territory around the sunken city of gold, Tom zoomed the *Sea Hound* to the surface. Here he contacted Enterprises by radio and gave his father a full report over the code scrambler.

Mr. Swift listened with grave concern and jotted down notes on Tom's undersea survey.

"I'll take Ebber's case up with the FBI," the scientist promised. "And frankly, Tom, I agree that it's high time for the United States to make an official claim to Aurum City. Your discovery and exploration of the area gives our government every right to take over."

Both Bud and Brian were jubilant as the *Sea Hound* plunged back toward the ocean bottom.

"That'll cool off those Brungarians in a hurry," Bud chortled. "They won't dare try any power plays once the Stars and Stripes are waving over Aurum City!"

Tom smiled, but inwardly he was still troubled. What was the story behind the mystery submarine they had found sunk near Aurum City? And what about Chow's foreboding over Longneck's smirking manner? The old Texan had proved before that he was a shrewd judge of human nature.

Chow, however, seemed to have forgotten his own warnings. As the *Sea Hound* approached Aurum City, the cook, smiling happily, wheeled a lunch cart into the flight compartment.

"Jest whomped up some tasty lil ole club steaks on my electronic range," Chow announced. "Prime Texas steer! After you passed me the good news over the intercom, boss, I figured we ought to celebrate!"

"Thanks, Chow!" Tom appreciatively sniffed the aroma of the steaks and French fried potatoes. "But let's not count our chickens too soon. The flag isn't officially hoisted yet over Aurum City."

"Don't worry, pal," Bud said as he forked up a juicy mouthful of steak. "With grub like this, nothing can stop us!"

There was little conversation as the group ate. When they had finished, the *Sea Hound* was berthed and Tom, Bud, and Chow entered the plastic dome. Work had gone on apace during their morning cruise. Freshly cleaned buildings of gold gleamed on all sides.

"Sure looks purty!" Chow said admiringly.

The three paused to watch a work crew cleaning off a pillared building near the entrance of the dome. Mel Flagler was operating the organ. As Mel swung the machine around, Tom suddenly

noticed that someone had left the entrance flap
to the plastic dome open.

"Hey!" he called out to a crewman. "Zip up
the—"

His warning was too late! The intake tube of
the organ pointed straight toward the dome opening!

There was a startling *whoosh* as the powerful
suction machine drew in a torrent of sea water.
Queer-looking fish and sea creatures came hurtling into the dome!

Pop! . . . Pop! . . . Pop!

They exploded right and left under the sudden release from the deep-ocean pressure! One—an enormous octopus—sent a shower of inky black fluid shooting in all directions!

"Smokin' rockets!" Bud gulped.

The work crew panicked in wild disorder! Mel Flagler caught a faceful of the repulsive black fluid through the open door of the cab. Tom, the only one to realize what had happened, raced toward the organ. Squeezing past the blinded Mel Flagler,

Queer-looking fish and sea creatures came hurtling into the dome

Tom managed to grab the switch lever and shut off the engine.

"Whew! What happened?" Mel gasped as he wiped his eyes.

Tom explained, then gazed at the city area nearest the dome entrance. What a mess it was! Not only were the streets flooded with sea water, but scraps of dead fish and other sea life were plastered everywhere. Over all lay a black film of octopus ink!

"Sure can't see no gold now!" Chow muttered disgustedly. *"Phooey!"*

"Never mind, old-timer," Tom called. "We'll clean it up—and then ourselves!"

For the next hour, the organ was kept busy removing the aftereffects of the disaster. Just as the submarine crews were settling back to their orderly work routine, Dick Strong—one of the two men assigned to guard Longneck Ebber—came rushing up to Tom.

"What's wrong?" Tom asked, noticing the worried look on the man's face.

Strong flushed shamefacedly. "Longneck Ebber is gone, skipper!" he panted. "I can't find him anywhere!"

CHAPTER XIV

THE RUSTY CHEST

THE NEWS that Longneck Ebber had disappeared filled Tom and his companions with dismay. It was not possible for him to have gone outside the air bubble. He would have drowned instantly. He must be hiding!

"How did he escape from you, Dick?" Tom asked tensely.

The guard explained that he had been walking his prisoner back from a work detail. "Then that accident happened—I mean the water pouring in and the fish exploding and all. I got that inky stuff in my face and couldn't watch Longneck. By the time I got through mopping myself off," Strong concluded, "he was gone!"

"And you've looked all over for him?"

"I can't find him anywhere in the city."

Tom was upset by the episode but wasted no

words in reproof. "The main thing now is to find out how Longneck pulled his vanishing act!"

Tom's mind was racing. Suppose that during the melee Ebber had somehow managed to signal an enemy submarine to pick him up!

On a hunch, Tom dashed aboard the *Sea Hound*. Hydrophone detectors had been rigged all around the bubble and hooked up to the ship's sonarscope. Tom queried the crewman on watch.

"Any blips on the scope recently?"

The sonarman shook his head. "All clear, skipper. There's been nothing within miles of here but fish."

Baffled, Tom returned to the dome. "I've checked off one hunch of mine," he said to Bud and Chow. He reported the sonarman's answer. "It means Ebber *must* be around here."

"Wal, personally," Chow growled, "I hope the varmint went outside an' drowned himself!"

"Wait!" Bud's eyes flashed as an idea occurred to him. "Suppose he sneaked aboard one of our submarines and hid? Maybe the guy can run a sub—and is waiting for a chance to hijack ours and take off!"

"Could be," Tom agreed. "We'd better search every ship from prow to stern!"

Word was passed to Mel Flagler, Zimby, and the crew captain of the last jetmarine to arrive. An intensive hunt was begun on all four vessels, including the *Sea Hound*. Every foot of compartment space was combed but no trace of the stowaway could be found.

"Longneck must be hiding out right in Aurum City then," Tom concluded, after hearing the reports from the other ships. "We'll make a street-by-street search."

Tom, Bud, and Chow formed one search party, while Brian, Mel, and Zimby each led another. The whole area within the dome was divided between the four groups.

"What if the polecat's packin' a gun?" Chow muttered uneasily as he and the two boys started off down one avenue.

"We disarmed Longneck when we first found him stowed away in the cargo hold," Bud replied. "If he had another gun concealed on him, he'd probably have used it before now."

Nevertheless, the trio proceeded cautiously. One by one, they probed through the long-abandoned villas and the palace. It gave them an eerie feeling, treading the ancient staircases and poking into empty, echoing rooms. Every trace of furnishings had vanished, long since rotted by the remorseless action of the sea.

"Wonder if there're any ghosts haunting these old buildings?" Bud remarked with a grin.

Tom chuckled wryly. "If there are, they must be pretty waterlogged by now."

Chow guffawed. "Brand my spooky pony, I'd kind o' like to meet one!"

When they finally reached the opposite side of the dome, after covering the whole street, the trio had still found no trace of Longneck Ebber. They paused before resuming the search on another avenue.

"Beats me where the varmint could've gone to," Chow grumbled.

"Same here," Tom said wearily. "Let's hope the others are having better luck."

He frowned as his eyes roved to a large rock— an outcropping from the canyon wall beyond the dome. The rock had a cavelike opening and looked as if it might once have been used as a storage place or granary.

"Say, look, fellows." Tom nudged his companions. "Maybe we should try that spot over there."

The words were hardly out of Tom's mouth when Longneck Ebber came strolling nonchalantly out of the cave!

"There's the rat!" Bud exploded.

"Wal, brand my trail-blazin' tea!" Chow glared at the skinny figure. "I reckon he heard you, boss, so he figgered he'd walk out first!"

Ebber wore his usual smirk. "Somethin' wrong, gents? You guys look peeved."

"Do you realize we've been looking all over for you?" Tom snapped angrily. "Next time you try pulling a fast one on your guard, Ebber, you're going to regret it! Maybe you'd like it better locked up in a ship's brig!"

"And maybe a slight going-over wouldn't do any harm, either!" Bud growled.

Longneck's smirk disappeared in a hurry. "No call to get sore," he said hastily. "Just thought I'd walk around a bit an' see if I could turn up any treasure." A sly look crept over his face as he added, "Matter of fact, I found somethin' kind o' interestin'."

Tom's eyes bored into him. "Such as?"

"Well, now, you think you're the first guy to find this sunken city, Swift," Longneck replied. "But I can prove different."

"Oh yes?" Bud retorted. "Go ahead and prove it then!"

Longneck grinned and jerked his thumb toward the cave. "Take a look yourself. There's a chest in there—a little rusty, maybe, but it sure can't be very old. An' it's heavy enough to hold plenty o' treasure, too. I couldn't even lift it!"

"How do you know it's not old?" Bud pressed.

Longneck chuckled, evidently enjoying the effect of his words. "There's none o' that fungus stuff on the chest, so figure it out, Buster! Someone must've left it here not too long ago."

"A deep-sea pirate, for instance?" Tom said meaningfully. "So you're finally going to tell us the truth about those skeletons."

He paused, hoping Ebber would go on to divulge whatever information he had.

But the suspect shrugged and gave the inventor a blank look. "I said I didn't know nothin' about any skeletons."

Not wishing to waste further time, Tom said flatly. "We'll take a look at that chest ourselves."

Taking out his pocket flashlight, Tom led the way into the cave. The interior of the stony chamber was dank and encrusted with the usual barnacles and sea growths. But his beam revealed a small rusty metal chest, completely free of ocean fungus.

"Great jumpin' Jehoshaphat!" Chow muttered.

Tom said nothing and tried the chest. It was small but heavy indeed. He lugged it outside the cave, into the daylike radiance of the dome lights. Tom opened the rusted hasp, using one of his pocket tools, then pried up the lid. Bud gave a whistle of astonishment.

Inside were a number of pieces broken off the gold statues—a sampling of Aurum City's treasures! There was also a sheet of paper, covered with a man's handwriting.

"What's it say, boss?" Chow asked anxiously.

Tom scanned the document with a frown. It was written in some foreign language. "I'm afraid I can't translate it, Chow," Tom murmured.

His voice sounded so glum and heavyhearted

that Bud and Chow both looked at Tom. He returned their glance grimly.

"Gosh, skipper," Bud blurted out, "you're not going to tell us this skinny rat was right about someone finding Aurum City before us?"

Tom shrugged unhappily. "Could be. This letter may even be an official claim to the city of gold by some explorer from another country. If so, our expedition is too late."

Bud and Chow stared in dismay at their young leader. The same thought ran through the minds of all three. Had the note been written by one of the men who lost their lives in the flooded submarine?

Tom felt sick with disappointment to think of the United States losing out after the efforts and hard work of himself and his crew!

A low chuckle from Longneck Ebber made Chow look around. He glared furiously at the man's gloating expression.

"You low-down sneakin' traitor!" the Texan bellowed. "I suppose you're plumb happy that Uncle Sam may lose this city! Wal, I'll wipe that ornery smirk off your face!"

Lunging forward, Chow lashed his gnarled fist square at Longneck Ebber's jaw!

CHAPTER XV

THE FOREIGN DETECTIVE

CHOW'S powerful blow caught Longneck Ebber by surprise. He reeled backward, but recovered quickly.

"Why, you fat old hash slinger!" Ebber snarled.

With a sudden rush, he charged forward and drove his fist hard into Chow's stomach. The cook let out an agonized grunt, momentarily paralyzed. Before he could get his breath, Ebber followed with an uppercut that rocked Chow's head!

Though half-dazed, the cook flailed out wildly. Ebber ducked and tried to upset Chow by grabbing one of his legs. Instead, Chow kicked upward, caught Ebber on the chin with the toe of his boot, and sent him sprawling.

The Texan, his blood really boiling by now, waited with clenched fists until Ebber got to his feet. Then he waded in!

"Wow! What a left!" Bud howled, as Chow

nailed his opponent with a roundhouse swing.

Ebber was gaunt and wiry, with whiplash muscles, but Chow's bulk concealed a reserve of rugged power from his hard years on the Western plains.

Chow fought cagily, wearing down his younger opponent. Most of Ebber's punches bounced harmlessly off the cook's leathery hide. Soon Ebber was puffing.

"Brand my six-shooters, you've had this comin' for a long time, Longneck!" Chow bellowed.

Opening up, he caught his adversary with a one-two combination, then drove another hard right to the prisoner's midriff. As Ebber tottered, Chow rocked his head with punches. Soon the struggle was over, with Longneck crumpling to his knees.

"L-lay off!" he pleaded, gasping for breath. "I'm licked! D-don't hit me again!"

Chow, who was puffing heavily himself, could only glare balefully at his beaten enemy.

"The winner by a technical knockout and still champion!" Bud sang out, raising Chow's right arm aloft.

"Reckon that smart aleck'll think twice afore he does any more smirkin'!" Chow panted.

Longneck had suffered a split lip, a generally battered-looking face, and a black eye that was rapidly swelling shut.

"Some fight, Chow! You really squared things for what happened to Lieutenant Cromwell." After a glance at Longneck's face, Tom added, "Longneck, I guess you're headed for sick bay."

The two boys marched the glum, discomfited loser back toward the *Sea Hound*. Chow strutted along behind, grinning triumphantly.

Tom hailed a crewman on the way and told him to notify the other search parties that Ebber had been found. A cluster of men gathered quickly.

"What happened, Ebber?" one gibed, realizing there had been a fight. "Run into a buzz saw?"

"A buzz saw named Chow Winkler!" Bud stated emphatically. The crewmen, who had been riled by Ebber's sneering manner, let out whoops of delight.

Reaching the *Sea Hound*, the boys turned Ebber over to Doc Simpson. Chow also required a few dabs of antiseptic and plaster.

Meanwhile, Tom and Bud went forward to the pilot's cabin. "What do we do now, pal?" Bud asked.

"First, I'll report the chest and note to Dad and see what he says. After that—well, what say we go back to that cave and hunt for other clues that might have been left by whoever planted the chest?"

"Smart idea."

Tom surfaced the *Sea Hound*, and radioed Enterprises. Dilling informed him that Mr. Swift had just taken off for Aurum City by seacopter.

"He has a man from the FBI with him, Tom,"

Dilling went on. "They'll bring back your prisoner."

"Good! But I wish Dad had brought along a linguist too," Tom replied. "We've found a mysterious foreign letter that needs translating."

"Maybe this FBI fellow can help you," Dilling said. "He's a Frenchman—on loan from the International Police Organization."

"You mean Interpol?"

"Right. From what your father told me, he has worked all over Europe and the Middle East and speaks many languages."

"Sounds like just the man we need," Tom said hopefully. "Okay, George—thanks!"

Signing off, Tom submerged again. He and Bud did not mention their proposed trip to the cave to any of the others, but set off at once. This time they carried powerful flashlights. When they reached the cave, Tom paused outside for another look at the objects in the chest.

"You know, Bud," he mused, picking up a clawed golden animal leg which had evidently been broken off a statue, "it might be a good idea to find out exactly where these pieces came from. If we find a statue that's—"

Suddenly Tom broke off with a gasp.

"What gives?" Bud asked, noting Tom's excitement.

"Take a look, Bud! This statue isn't solid gold after all!" Tom pointed to the fractured surface of the metal. The piece had an inner core with a strange yellowish sheen. This was overlaid with a shell of gold.

"Tom," said Bud in awe, "I remember your saying the stuff might not be twenty-four-carat when we cleaned off that first building. But what's this metal inside?"

Tom shook his head, puzzled. "An alloy probably. I'll have to analyze it."

"What about the temples and palaces around here?" Bud asked. "Do you suppose they're all like this?"

Tom snapped his fingers. "We can soon find out. Let's take a look at the column that fell over!"

Excitedly Tom and Bud rushed back to the spot where they had had their close brush with a near fatal accident. The column still lay where it had fallen. Before the boys were halfway there, there minds were diverted by a loud *crack* overhead.

"Ouch! What's that?" Bud asked.

His eyes widened in dismay as they followed Tom's glance upward. A long fracture showed in the plastic dome! As they gaped, another crack appeared with a loud report. An instant later a chunk of the plastic broke off and came clattering down, narrowly missing a crewman.

"Good grief! The dome's breaking up!" Bud gasped.

Tom was horrified. The enclosure was needed to maintain a stable atmosphere—without it, the osmotic air conditioner would no longer function properly! The atmosphere inside the air bubble would become unbearably humid!

"What's causing the breakup, Tom?" Bud cried, as shouts of alarm rose from all sides. More cracks appeared and another fragment broke off.

"Must be the organ!" Tom guessed, sizing up the situation fast. Breaking into a run, Tom dashed toward Mel Flagler's work crew. He cupped his hands and shouted, "Turn off the de-organic-izer!"

His words were drowned in a sudden fusillade of noise overhead. The dome, weakened by the cracks, was caving in completely! Whole sheets and chunks of the plastic ceiling came raining down in a deadly barrage as the yelling crewmen flattened themselves or ducked for cover.

The breakup continued for several moments. When Tom finally dared raise his head, he saw that little was left of the dome except the slender, shiny framework of magnesium struts.

"Tom! Are you okay?" Bud called.

The young inventor nodded grimly. "But the crew must've taken a beating. Go get Doc, will you, Bud? I'll see how bad things are!"

Ignoring his own cuts and bruises, Tom hurried to check on his men. Nearly all had been hit by the falling fragments. One man was unconscious. But fortunately only a few had suffered serious injury.

"Shall I rig a stretcher for Pete?" Mel Flagler asked, referring to the unconscious victim.

Tom shook his head, after checking Pete's pulse. "Better not move him till Doc gets here." Summoning the bleeding crewmen, he added, "Line up here, fellows, so we can get those cuts attended to fast!"

Doc arrived on the double, and after reviving Pete, ordered him put to bed. Then he hastily took over the job, which Tom had already begun, of treating and bandaging the injured men.

"I still can't figure it out," Bud said, walking up to Tom with a puzzled air. "Why should the organ make the dome go to pieces?"

Tom picked up several of the plastic fragments and examined them. "This stuff's gone brittle as glass," he muttered. "Apparently the S-Co unit caused a chemical change in the plastic wherever the intake was carelessly aimed toward the dome. Once an internal strain was set up in the material, it was just a question of time before the whole dome cracked up."

"Oh, fine!" Bud said gloomily. "Does that mean we can't ever use the organ inside an air dome?"

"Depends on whether or not I can correct it," Tom replied. "We'd better stop work, anyhow, till we get a new dome."

"Turn off the de-organic-izer!" Tom shouted

After adjusting the air conditioner to compensate as much as possible for the changed conditions, Tom partly disassembled his spectromarine selector. He had the electronic controls of the S-Co unit moved into his laboratory.

Chow, entering the compartment an hour later, said cheerfully, "How about forcin' down a lil nourishment, boss?"

"No thanks, Chow. Too busy." Tom, hard at work on his problem, scarcely looked up.

"Shucks now, you can take some o' this nice, hot chicken gumbo soup. I declare if you don't, I'll have to spoon-feed you!"

Grinning at Chow's cajolery, Tom broke off long enough to gulp down the soup. Then he plunged back to work.

The problem was not too difficult. The young inventor had already analyzed a piece of the broken plastic under his spectroscope to determine the exact chemical change that had taken place. The selector circuit of the S-Co would need an automatic control to prevent it from acting on any substance having the same carbon-hydrogen-oxygen ratio as Tomasite.

The tedious work would come in the actual rewiring of the electronic assembly. By midnight Tom finished the job and with a yawn turned in.

"Success?" Bud asked the next morning as Tom opened his eyes.

His chum nodded and soon the two were installing the altered S-Co unit in the organ.

Presently the sonarman stuck his head out of the *Sea Hound*. "Sub approaching, skipper, from the northwest!"

Tom grinned happily. "Dad!"

His guess proved correct. Within twenty minutes the newly arrived seacopter lay berthed alongside the *Sea Hound* and Tom was exchanging a warm greeting with his father.

"Son, I want you to meet Henry Stern, who's working with the FBI," Mr. Swift said.

The lean, wiry man shook hands with Tom. "My real name is Henri Austére," he explained with a smile, "but I'm using an Anglicized version for the time being."

"I'm sure you can help us a lot, sir," Tom said eagerly.

After introducing the French agent to Bud Barclay and Lieutenant Fraser, Tom suggested that they hold an immediate conference aboard the *Sea Hound*. Here he broke the news about the mysterious chest. He showed the letter found in it to the agent. Mr. Swift glanced at it with a puzzled frown.

"Can you translate it, Mr. Stern?" Tom asked.

A tense and anxious silence followed as the detective from Interpol examined the letter.

CHAPTER XVI

AN AMAZING ALLOY

THE SUSPENSE was almost unbearable to the Swifts. Presently the Interpol agent glanced up at Tom. His eyes were grim and troubled.

"Bad news?"

Henry Stern nodded. "I'm afraid so. This was written by three submarine explorers from Brungaria—"

As Tom was about to interrupt in surprise, Stern added, "They used the old historical spelling of their country's name, which is probably why you didn't recognize it. I'll read you what's written here."

He proceeded to translate aloud:

> WE, THE UNDERSIGNED, HAVE DIS-
> COVERED THIS SUNKEN CITY AND
> HEREBY OFFICIALLY CLAIM IT FOR
> THE IMPERIAL BRUNGARIAN GOVERN-

MENT. WE HOPE TO RETURN SAFELY
BY SUBMARINE TO OUR NATIVE LAND.
BUT IF ANY ACCIDENT SHOULD BE-
FALL US, THIS LETTER WILL PROVE
THAT WE WERE THE ORIGINAL DIS-
COVERERS OF THIS SITE. WE ARE CON-
FIDENT THAT ALL OTHER NATIONS
WILL RESPECT BRUNGARIA'S PRIOR
RIGHTS.

(signed) FRITZ BRANOV
YANNOS GURR
IGOR JADENKO

The listeners were stunned.

"Then . . . then it's definite that our expedition is too late," Bud said falteringly after a moment of dead silence. "The United States can't
take over Aurum City?"

"I'm afraid not, Bud," Mr. Swift replied
quietly. "Even if those explorers died before re-
porting their discovery, the only honorable thing
our country can do is to acknowledge their claim."

Lieutenant Fraser gave a tight-lipped nod. "We
can hardly expect foreign powers to respect other
countries' rights unless we do the same," he muttered. "But it sure goes against the grain to hand
all this over to Brungaria!"

Bud got up and paced angrily about the compartment. "What a rotten break!" he gritted.

Henry Stern spoke up sympathetically. "I re-

gret this unhappy news, gentlemen. But you will
understand that I am here as an international
police official and representative of the FBI. We
must now concern ourselves with the prisoner,
Longneck Ebber."

"Quite right," Mr. Swift said. "Do you think it
best that he be taken back to the United States
immediately?"

Stern shrugged. "His official arrest can be de-
layed if you wish, *mon ami,*" he replied. "Once
Ebber is taken into federal custody and charged
with his crimes, he will of course have a right to
talk to a lawyer. One of them might leak the story
to the newspapers. If that happens, your work here
at the city of gold will doubtless become head-
line news."

The Interpol man paused, his eyes shifting
from Mr. Swift to Tom. "But perhaps that no
longer matters?" he questioned.

"Probably not," Mr. Swift conceded. "However, until this Brungarian claim is officially veri-
fied, it might be wise to avoid publicity. What do
you think, son?"

Tom had been silent and thoughtful, his keen
mind already leaping ahead to other problems.
"It wouldn't hurt to play safe, Dad," he agreed.
"To tell the truth, though, Ebber's been nothing
but a nuisance and I'd sure like to get him away
from here."

Turning to Mr. Stern, Tom added, "Suppose

you interrogate him, sir. Ebber may be hiding
something we don't know yet. If you can pry any
more out of him, that may help us decide what to
do."

Stern nodded approvingly. "A wise suggestion."
His tanned face broke into a faint grin. "Sometimes, by patient questioning, one can learn more
than a suspect wishes to reveal—*n'est ce pas?*"

"Right!" Tom smiled and stood up. "Bud,
would you please take Mr. Stern to the prisoner?"

"Sure. Be glad to."

"And tell Strong and Ehler to stand by in case
Longneck tries pulling any more fast ones!"

As Bud went off with the Interpol agent, the
conference broke up.

Tom turned to his father. "In the meantime,
Dad, there's something I want to show you. It
may be important."

There was a hint of mystery and suppressed
excitement in Tom's manner. Highly curious,
Mr. Swift accompanied his son into the air dome.
The scientist was amazed at his first close glimpse
of Aurum City's golden buildings and statuary.

"What a thrilling sight!" he gasped. "Tom, this
historical treasure should be open to scholars and
sightseers of all countries!"

"You're right, Dad," Tom said wryly. "Let's
hope the Brungarians feel the same way."

Tom led his father down a splendid avenue,
lined with columns, toward the cave. Here he

showed him one of the broken-off metal pieces from the chest. Tom pointed to the core under the gold overlay.

"Ever seen a metal like this before, Dad?"

Mr. Swift examined the sample. A frown creased his brow. Taking out a high-powered, double-lensed pocket magnifier, he studied the surface of fracture.

"Hmm. This is certainly new to me, Tom. It's an alloy, of course—probably with a gold base, although it seems very lightweight."

"Good guess, Dad." Tom explained that he had had a rough analysis made that morning. "This alloy does contain gold, but also an unusual combination of other elements, including scandium, rubidium, and beryllium."

Mr. Swift was astonished to hear of such a complex alloy being used by an ancient people. "They surely couldn't have developed it themselves," he reasoned.

"Exactly!" Tom's eyes gleamed. "Which means this alloy must occur in nature, Dad. And it must have been mined in huge quantities if they could use it for building this whole city!"

Tom was sure this was the case, since he had checked the toppled column and found it to be composed of the same gold-shelled alloy.

After explaining that he had run some quick metallurgical tests of the alloy that morning, Tom sprang his big surprise.

"Dad, this alloy may be just the metal you need to solve your rocket problem! It's lightweight, very strong, and seems to have properties similar to the alloy you're now using!"

Mr. Swift's face lit up at the news. "Tom, that's more than I dared hope for! Why, with a supply of this alloy, we could easily fulfill our rocket contract!"

Then his eager look faded quickly after a moment's reflection. "I'm afraid we're forgetting, son, that Aurum City is no longer an American possession," he murmured. "Even if it were, it would be wicked to destroy such a legacy from the past—to build rockets or for any other reason."

Tom grinned. "I agree. But I'm not talking about melting down these buildings and statues."

"What are you proposing?" Mr. Swift asked.

"That we find out where the alloy came from!" Tom's voice took on a fresh note of excitement. "There's no sign of any mine or quarry near Aurum City, Dad, so both this alloy and the gold must have been brought from a distance. What's to prevent us from finding the source?"

Tom's reasoning brought a surge of hope to Mr. Swift. "You're right, son! It's certainly worth a try."

"I didn't have time to finish testing the alloy," Tom went on. "Let's work on it now."

Mr. Swift agreed enthusiastically. Father and

son hurried back to Tom's laboratory aboard the *Sea Hound*. On Mr. Swift's suggestion, they first made a mass spectrographic analysis of the gold.

"Most interesting," the elder scientist concluded after making various calculations. "This gold has the same isotope ratio as Peruvian gold."

"*Peruvian* gold!" Tom pounced on this clue. "That's further evidence to back up the Inca legend!" he pointed out.

Mr. Swift nodded thoughtfully. "Your retroscope may help us uncover other clues, son. I brought it along, by the way."

"Swell, Dad!"

The two scientists now proceeded to analyze the alloy more precisely. Their amazement grew when they discovered that it also contained faint radioactive traces of three different transuranium elements.

The next step was to test the alloy for corrosion resistance, elasticity, tensile strength, toughness, and other properties—not only under normal conditions but when heated to rocket blast temperatures.

The elder and younger Swifts looked more like brothers as they bent over the laboratory worktable. Both had the same lean build and keen, deep-set blue eyes. But Tom Jr., rangy and still growing, was an inch taller than his father.

When they finished their experiment, Tom Sr. was glowing with enthusiasm. "No question about it," he declared, doffing his lab apron. He began to scour the chemical stains off his hands. "This alloy tops anything I had hoped to find. As a rocket metal, it's even better than our present alloy!"

Young Tom was already mentally evaluating their chances of locating the metal's source. "In view of those radioactive traces, Dad, I believe the alloy may come from somewhere near our under-sea helium wells," he conjectured.

Mr. Swift agreed. But he shook his head worriedly at the job confronting them. "Even if we find the source," he pointed out, "it will be a stupendous operation to mine at such depths."

Again Tom had a ready answer. "Not with my new selectrol filtration pump," he said quietly.

Mr. Swift's eyebrows shot up in surprise. "Another new invention, son?"

"Actually I worked it out some time ago," Tom replied, "but I laid it aside when we took on this gold-city project."

The new device, Tom explained, was somewhat like a centrifuge used for spinning off cream from milk. "As you know, Dad," he went on, "when it's spun around, the cream—being the lightest part of the milk—is not thrown to the outside of the whirling mixture, and is drained off separately from the rest of the liquid."

"But this method, of course, works only with liquid mixtures," Mr. Swift remarked, "or suspensions which can be separated into a 'heavy' and a 'light' part, and has no effect on chemical *solutions*. For instance, a centrifuge couldn't remove the dissolved salt from sea water. So how can your invention separate the alloy from the rest of the dissolved ocean matter?"

"By a repelatron radiator at the center of the pump," Tom replied. "This would be tuned to repel only the alloy—in other words, force it to the outside of the sea water which is whirling around inside the pump casing."

Grabbing a pencil, Tom sketched his device. The spinning pump, or impeller, would be horizontal. A steady flow of sea water would be sucked in at the top and leave through a pipe at the bottom. The desired substance for which the repelatron was tuned—in this case, the alloy—would be piped off into a collection tank at one side.

This, Tom continued, formed only the "first stage" of his selectrol pump. There were also two other impeller stages to make sure that none of the desired substance was lost.

"Wonderful!" Mr. Swift flashed his son a warm, admiring smile. "Tom, you never stop surprising me with the rabbits you pull out of your hat. This is certainly just what we need for mining the alloy!"

Both looked up as Bud came bursting into the tiny laboratory compartment.

"Get set for a big surprise!" he exclaimed. "I think we've just discovered a hoax!"

CHAPTER XVII

UNDERSEA PROSPECTORS

AT BUD'S heels was the French detective, Henry
Stern. He was carrying both the Brungarian letter
and the metal chest, now empty.

"As Bud says, Messieurs Swift," he announced,
"I suspect that we have here a very clever hoax."

Tom shot the agent a startled glance. "Are you
telling us the chest is a fake—that it was planted
in the cave to fool us?"

"Let us say I am very suspicious," Stern replied.
"In my opinion, Ebber could easily have played
such a trick. I understand that he was the one who
found the chest—after disappearing for over an
hour."

Tom nodded thoughtfully. "That's right."

"But how could he have smuggled it into
Aurum City?" Mr. Swift objected. "Ebber had
nothing with him when found aboard, did he?"

"He pulled a gun, but we disarmed him," Bud

explained. "There was nothing of importance on Longneck when we searched him."

"And he couldn't have concealed an object as big as that chest," Mr. Swift added.

"In its present form—*non*," the Frenchman said. "But you will notice that the chest is made of thin separate panels."

Tom's eyes glinted. "You mean Ebber brought the chest here broken down in sections, then assembled it inside the cave?"

Stern nodded. "Exactly. He could have had the pieces hidden in the hold when he stowed away. Also the letter—given Ebber by the man called Decko. He was just waiting for a chance to plant both of them."

"The theory makes sense, Dad!" Tom snapped his fingers. "Ebber could have welded the chest panels together with a midget electronic tool powered by a pen-sized solar battery. It wouldn't have been any trouble for him to have picked up one around here."

Mr. Swift nodded, then asked Stern, "Have you checked for Ebber's fingerprints on the chest or its contents?"

"His prints were on the chest, but of course he admits handling that in the cave," the detective replied. "The metal pieces inside had been wiped clean. Surely those alleged Brungarian explorers would not have done so!"

Tom's mind worked fast. "There's one sure

way to find out if the chest is a fake," he told the others. "My electronic retroscope!"

Tom led the way as the group hurried excitedly to the seacopter which Mr. Swift had piloted to Aurum City. Within minutes, the retroscope had been set up and turned on, with the scanner aimed at one of the chest's welded seams.

The master time dial of the retroscope showed that despite the rusty appearance of the chest, the welding was scarcely twenty-four hours old!

"You've proved it, Tom!" Bud whooped.

"Right, Bud. The welding job was done just about the time Longneck Ebber was in the cave."

To make their case legally secure, Mr. Swift suggested that they try to find the welding tool. Tom and Bud rushed off with powerful flashlights to search the cave.

"While they're gone," said Stern, "I'll get busy too."

Twenty minutes later all three returned to Mr. Swift, grinning in triumph. Tom ordered Ebber to be brought aboard the *Sea Hound* for questioning.

"Don't you guys ever give up?" Ebber greeted the group with his usual smirk.

Tom smiled calmly. "Just one last question, Longneck. Ever seen this before?"

He signaled Bud, who pulled out a tiny pencil-sized welding device—holding it carefully with a handkerchief.

Longneck Ebber's face turned a sickly greenish hue. Stammering, he tried to cover his confusion.

"I d-don't even know what it is!"

Bud broke into a contemptuous laugh. "Don't you? Then we'll tell you, wise guy! It's a miniature electric welder—the tool you used to rig up a phony chest!"

Henry Stern opened his portable fingerprint kit and held up two photographs of prints—one marked FBI, the other obviously just made. The detective turned to Ebber.

"So you have never seen this before—eh, monsieur? Then perhaps you will explain how the prints on the articles *inside* the chest happen to match yours!"

Ebber slumped against the bulkhead, pale and sweating. But he refused to talk.

"Never mind," Henry Stern told him. "We need no confession. With this evidence, you will most assuredly be convicted as a traitor to your own country!"

Bud gave Ebber a withering look, then cried out, "Do you all realize what this means? Uncle Sam can now claim Aurum City!"

The Swifts cheered and Henry Stern wrung the hands of all the Americans except Ebber. "I am proud that France was able to be of assistance in helping you stake the claim for your nation," he said with a slight bow.

Mr. Swift surfaced his own seacopter to radio

Shopton the good news. Harlan Ames joyfully promised to contact the State and Defense departments at once.

Two days later a division of United States Navy submarines arrived at the site. A new dome had been delivered and erected, and a large section of the ancient spot was gleaming. Old Glory was officially unfurled over Aurum's tallest building, the palace, and the sleek Navy undersea craft set up a regular defense patrol around the city.

"Brand my red, white, and blue prairie flowers! Don't that flag look good up there?" Chow chuckled and rubbed his hands in glee.

"It sure does," Tom agreed with a grin. "But the cleanup work is still only half done—and now we have a new job ahead of us."

"What's that, boss?"

"The job of finding where the alloy came from that was used in building this city," Tom explained. "We must locate the source and mine the alloy for Dad to use in filling his new rocket contract."

"What you callin' this new stuff?" Chow asked.

"Neo-aurium. That means 'like gold.' "

With the city now safely guarded by the United States Navy and work proceeding in round-the-clock shifts, Tom surfaced and radioed Enterprises. He briskly issued a series of orders based on a plan talked over with his father.

A cargo jet bearing another plastic dome was

to be rushed at once to Aurum. Also, the *Sky Queen,* Tom's giant atomic jet plane known as the Flying Lab, was to be flown to a spot near the helium wells. Tom and his group would rendezvous with it there before diving on their sub-ocean prospecting trip to find the source of the mystery alloy.

The *Sky Queen* was to carry in its huge cargo hold a deep-sea elevator, a repelatron, a special caterpillar tractor-trailer rig, and Tom's new selectrol filtration pump.

"Got that list, George?" Tom asked as he finished checking off the items.

"Roger!" Dilling replied. "And I'll tell 'em to add other tools and equipment."

"Okay. And another thing—Henry Stern is taking Longneck Ebber back in Dad's seacopter. Tell Ames to meet them. Dad will stay here with us for the time being."

"Right, skipper. And good luck!"

Tom signed off and the *Sea Hound* plunged back to Aurum City. Within an hour the other seacopter was ready to depart. Henry Stern shook hands all around before stepping aboard with his prisoner.

"Rest assured, *mes amis,* that Ebber will soon be safely behind bars," he told the Swifts.

"Thanks for your help," Mr. Swift replied. "We'll keep our fingers crossed that you and Ames can round up his confederates."

Tom added a *bon voyage*. Moments later, the seacopter zoomed upward and was lost to view.

Shortly afterward, the *Sea Hound* darted off on a westerly course. Aboard were Tom and his father, Bud, Brian Fraser, Chow, and the rest of the crew. Reaching the latitude and longitude of the rendezvous position, the *Sea Hound* surfaced to await the Flying Lab. At one o'clock that afternoon, as Chow was clearing away the lunch dishes, a silvery swept-wing plane came jetting out of the blue, its vapor trail pluming across the sky.

"The *Sky Queen!*" Bud yelled.

Hank Sterling's voice came over the radio. "Greetings, you old sea dogs! Where do we dump this stuff?"

"Right here," Tom replied. "Elevator first."

Its jet lifters working, the *Sky Queen* hovered in low, alongside the *Sea Hound*. The cargo hatch of the plane was opened. Then a heavy anchor frame, attached to twin steel cables, was lowered into the water. There was a shrill whine as the cables unreeled. Presently a red light flashed in the plane, indicating that the frame had touched bottom.

The elevator was then rigged, with its guides clamped around the cables.

"Okay, skipper. What next?" Hank signaled.

"The trailer," Tom answered.

Hank's crew began loading the disassembled axles and frame onto the elevator. Meanwhile,

Tom, Bud, Brian, and Mr. Swift went topside on the *Sea Hound*. The two boys climbed into Fat Man suits. At a signal from Tom, the elevator platform was lowered to the surface of the water. All four stepped aboard.

The elevator had its own small repelatron. Mr. Swift opened the control switch as Brian unhooked the winch line from the *Sky Queen*. The elevator platform was now supported only by repulsion ray as a bubble started forming in the water.

Then he eased off on the switch, allowing the elevator to sink. As it dropped below the surface, the air bubble, fully developed, enclosed the elevator.

Down the group went, thousands of feet. A light switched on automatically as the greenish water darkened around them.

In ten minutes they reached bottom. Tom and Bud in their Fat Man suits shoved the first load of tractor-trailer parts off the elevator and into the water.

"Ah! Now the work begins!" Bud remarked over his suit's sonarphone.

"Hop to it, pal!" Tom replied with a grin.

Working with their mechanical Fat Man arms, the boys started to assemble the trailer.

Meanwhile, Mr. Swift opened the repelatron switch again. As the air bubble expanded, thus increasing buoyancy, the elevator rose to the surface. On the next trip, the rest of the trailer assembly was carried down.

Axles, frame, and deck plates were bolted together, forming a flat-bed trailer. By the time the boys had finished, the elevator was down again, bringing the undersea repelatron.

Tom and Bud mounted it on the flat deck of the trailer. Next came a small osmotic air conditioner. Tom switched on the atomic power to operate this unit and the repelatron. A spacious air bubble quickly formed around the trailer. At last the boys were able to climb out of their Fat Man suits.

"Whew!" Tom wiped the sweat from his brow. "Those pantograph arms are fine, but I think I can work better with a wrench in my bare hand."

"Same here!" Bud chuckled.

A high-powered midget tractor was taken down and the boys hooked this up to the trailer. Last came the selectrol filtration pump, which Bud called the SFP. To save space, Tom had decided to use only the first stage. This, too, was mounted on the trailer deck. Finally, Mr. Swift and Brian Fraser came down.

"What an amazing setup!" the lieutenant commented admiringly as he watched the boys tighten the last bolts on the strange-looking rig.

"Tom's own idea." Mr. Swift smiled proudly.

In effect, Tom had created a tractorized air dome in which the occupants could move about freely over the ocean floor as they prospected for the neo-aurium.

"We may as well start our sampling right here, Dad," Tom decided.

He adjusted the SFP controls to the chemical make-up of neo-aurium. Then his hand flicked on the control lever and the pump whirred into action. After ten minutes a few coarse golden-colored grains had collected in the SFP's tank.

"Undersea desert prospectors panning for gold, that's us!" Bud joked.

"We'll never get rich at this rate," Tom said wryly.

"At least you've proved your theory, son," Mr. Swift remarked, looking affectionately at Tom. "There's neo-aurium around here, although we may be miles from the source."

At the moment they were located near the foot of the undersea mountain which ran past the helium wells. Bud climbed into the tractor seat and began skirting along the hill. A continuous flow of water was drawn through the SFP. After traveling another half mile, Tom noticed that the grains of alloy began showing up more plentifully.

"We must be getting closer!" he exclaimed.

Suddenly Brian's eye fell on the pump pressure gauge. The needle was flickering past the red danger point!

"Hold it, Tom!" he cried, grabbing wildly for the control lever.

The next moment the pump casing exploded! Tom, Brian, and Mr. Swift were knocked off their feet by the blast. Bud, though dazed, was saved by his grip on the tractor steering wheel. He dismounted hastily and switched off the pump which was spurting sea water in all directions.

"Anyone hurt?" he cried.

Brian's scalp had been grazed by a flying piece of the shattered pump casing. But otherwise the victims were merely stunned by the shock wave inside the dome. Bud helped them up.

Tom, embarrassed and worried, said shamefacedly, "We're lucky. A direct hit from that pump casing would have killed any one of us!"

Bud felt sorry for him. Slapping his chum on the back, he said, "Guess you live right, Tom."

"Thanks." Tom quickly assessed the damage. Fortunately, the repelatron and air conditioner were still functioning. The SFP was also intact, except for the shattered pump casing and some twisted impeller blades.

"At least the machinery wasn't smashed," the young inventor murmured. "But we'll need a repair job before we can do any more prospecting."

Tom took the wheel of the tractor and drove the air-dome rig back to the elevator. He and the others ascended to the surface, bringing with them the pump impeller and the pieces of casing. Hank Sterling's crew lowered a cable ladder so the four could climb aboard the Flying Lab.

*A moment after Brian's warning, the pump
casing exploded!*

"What happened?" Hank Sterling asked.

Tom explained and showed him the pump casing. It had shattered into six large pieces—each cleanly fractured. "Think these could be welded strongly enough to stand up under pressure?"

"Sure," said Hank, after a moment's study. "In fact, I can make the casing stronger than it was before."

"You're elected," Bud put in with a relieved grin. "Boy, I could see us all walking the ocean floor, waiting for a new one to be flown out here!"

While Hank did the welding, Tom and his father forged and machined some new impeller blades in the *Sky Queen*'s amazingly well-equipped laboratory. In an hour the group was ready to descend again.

Boarding the elevator, they shot downward. But gradually it slowed to a halt. Tom eased off on the repelatron power in order to shrink the air bubble as much as possible. The elevator sank a bit, then stopped again.

"What's wrong?" Brian asked.

"I don't know," Tom replied.

Deciding to surface for inspection, Tom opened the switch. The elevator rose slightly, then stopped with a jolt and refused to budge.

"Good night!" Bud cried out. "We're stuck!"

The prospectors were trapped a mile below the ocean's surface!

er it," Bud said, breathing easie
ystery was solved.

CHAPTER XVIII

AN ENEMY THREAT

"GOOD thing we brought along our Fat Man suits," Bud remarked, trying not to show his nervousness.

Brian Fraser also looked a trifle pale. But he remained calm, confident that Tom Jr. and Tom Sr. would soon find a way out of the frightening predicament. Both father and son were studying the situation.

The deep-sea elevator was a larger and later model of the one Tom had created for work at the helium wells. Its platform was supported by magnesium struts with the cable guides extending high overhead.

"Hey! I see what's stopping us!" Tom cried suddenly, pointing upward.

One of the twin cables had kinked and was being pulled out of plumb by an enormous mass of floating seaweed! The cable guide was unable to get past the obstruction.

"We can free it," Bud said, breathing easier now that the mystery was solved.

"We may still have trouble rising if the kink is permanent," Mr. Swift cautioned. "And we still don't know what's preventing us from descending," he added in a troubled voice.

"At least we can take a whack at that seaweed," Tom said. "Into your suit, Bud!"

The two boys climbed inside their steel eggs and stepped off the elevator into the water. Trimming their suits' ballast tanks, they rose to a point level with the fouled cable.

"Ugh! What a mess!" Bud grunted, sweeping the tangled ocean growth away from his view plate.

"People pay money for this stuff and eat it, don't forget." Tom chuckled. "We should have forks with us."

"Pitchforks, you mean," Bud retorted over his sonarphone.

Using their pantograph arms, the boys ripped and tore at the matted weeds. They seemed to extend for hundreds of feet beyond the cable.

"We're lucky this mass didn't drift any closer," Tom commented. "It might have fouled the whole elevator!"

In ten minutes they managed to free the cable. The seaweed quickly drifted away, propelled by the deep-ocean current. But, as Mr. Swift had feared, it had put a permanent kink in the cable.

"Can we straighten it?" Bud asked dubiously.

"We'll soon find out," Tom replied. "Rev your suit motor up to full torque."

Gripping the cable with their Fat Man claws, the boys applied a powerful leverage. Bit by bit, they straightened the cable into shape.

"That should do it," Tom decided.

When they re-entered the elevator air bubble and doffed their suits, they found Mr. Swift replacing an inspection plate in the floor of the platform.

"Your dad has just found the reason why we couldn't go down," Brian told Tom.

The elder inventor explained that several of the lead ballast bars were missing from their racks under the platform. Without this extra weight to help them sink, the elevator was not heavy enough to counteract the air bubble's buoyancy—even with the repelatron tuned low.

"Well, I'll be a dopey duck," Bud groaned. "Like trying to fish without a sinker!"

"Those bars were certainly in place when we rigged the trailer," Tom said with a frown.

"The rack clip came loose," Mr. Swift reported.

Bud chuckled. "We should get Chow down here and have him serve some of his heavy dinners!" As Tom winced at the gag, Bud added, "Seriously, pal—want me to go topside in a Fat Man and get some more ballast?"

"We can all go if that kink's straightened

enough," Tom replied. "Let's find out. Going up, everybody!"

He opened the repelatron switch. As the air bubble expanded, the elevator rose smoothly to the surface. Hank's crew provided some extra lead bars and the trouble was soon corrected. This time they descended to the ocean floor without difficulty.

Again the group boarded the tractorized air dome. Tom and his father quickly installed the welded casing and new impeller blades. Then Bud took the wheel and drove back to the spot where the pump had blown up.

"For Pete's sake keep an eye on that pressure gauge, pal!" Bud warned jokingly.

"I'll watch it like a hawk," Tom promised.

He started the SFP as the trailer resumed its slow crawl along the mountainside. The air bubble was like a ghostly moving blob of light in the murky ocean depths. On their right, the mountain loomed as a black mass.

"Out of our way, Buster!" Bud snarled at a weird electric-blue fish that swam into the glare of their searchlight.

The monster glared back with its bulging eyes, then weaved away out of view.

"How're we coming back there?" Bud called, throwing a glance over his shoulder.

"Getting more neo-aurium," Tom reported. "Keep going in the same direction."

Tom, Mr. Swift, and Brian Fraser were huddled around the collection tank, watching intently as the golden grains filtered down from the pump. Though the yield was encouraging, both Tom and his father felt they still had not reached the source.

"It has to be *somewhere* around here," Tom said tensely.

After several more miles of prospecting, a much heavier deposit of neo-aurium began showing up in the tank. Soon the pump was showering off a steady stream of the glistening alloy!

"Wow!" Tom exclaimed enthusiastically. "Dad, this may be it!"

Mr. Swift nodded. Smiling, he gripped his son's arm. Brian, too, watched with an air of barely controlled excitement.

Gradually the yield of neo-aurium began to lessen again. Realizing that they were passing out of range, Tom ordered Bud to circle back. This time, they veered farther out along the shelving slopes of the mountainside. By observing the rate at which the golden grains were being deposited in the tank, Tom fixed the point of maximum concentration.

"The mine must have been right about here!" he declared. "We'll find it if we have to blast open this whole mountainside!"

Bud braked the rig to a halt and leaped off the tractor to see for himself. The tank was heaped with glittering particles of neo-aurium!

"Hurray! We've struck it rich!" he cried out.

Mr. Swift grinned as the boys did a quick jig. "It may take some digging to find the mother lode," he reminded them. "I suggest that you continue your search in the seacopter."

"Aren't you coming?" Tom asked.

"Not this time, son. I want to work on the new alloy in the lab, so I'll know just how to proceed when you find that mine."

Eager to tackle the job ahead, Tom drove back to the deep-sea elevator. He and Bud hastily donned Fat Man suits and began dismantling the tractor rig. Mr. Swift and Brian ferried each load up to the surface.

At last the boys were able to take off their steel diving gear and ride up with the last of the trailer assembly. The sparkling sunshine was a welcome change from the oppressive ocean depths.

As they breathed in hearty lungfuls of air, a crewman shouted from the *Sky Queen*. "Radio message coming through from Shopton! Want to catch it?"

Tom and Mr. Swift climbed aboard and hurried to the Flying Lab's radio compartment. Harlan Ames was calling over the scrambler.

"We finally got a lead on that man Decko," the security chief reported. "An undercover source tipped off the FBI."

"Any chance of nailing him?" Tom asked over the microphone.

"Not much. It appears that Decko has slipped out of the country." Ames's voice became tense. "Now here's the bad part. Before he left, Decko was really burned because Judson and Ebber had been caught. So he swore he'd get you and your dad himself."

"Any idea what he has in mind?"

"No, but for goodness' sake watch your step!" Ames pleaded. "Decko's ruthless and he's playing for high stakes. He'll stop at nothing!"

"We'll take every precaution, Harlan," Mr. Swift promised. "In the meantime, keep us informed, but don't mention the threat to Mrs. Swift or Sandy."

"Not a word. But please—play it safe!"

A bustle of activity followed as Tom prepared for the mine hunt by submarine. Extra tools, including undersea cutting torches and rock drills, were transferred from the *Sky Queen* to the seacopter. Improved models of Tom Jr.'s Damonscope and Tom Sr.'s underwater metal detector were also installed in the *Sea Hound*.

The Damonscope was an ultrasensitive device for detecting radioactive ore by recording ultraviolet fluorescence on a moving strip of film. Tom had used it to locate a fabulous lode of Swiftonium in South America.

The underwater detector, which had once guided Tom to a sunken rocket sent by his space friends, did its probing by means of a special type of ultrahigh-frequency beam. The change in frequency of the reflected signal showed the molecular nature of the substance causing the echo.

While Bud supervised the loading, Tom installed extra-powerful scanning lights in the *Sea Hound*.

"Boy! How can we miss with a setup like this!" Bud gloated.

"We *can't*—I hope!" Tom said with a grin.

By now, the quick darkness of the tropics was settling over the ocean. Chow reminded the Swifts and their friends that they had not eaten for a long time. They agreed, ate a good supper, and had a restful night's sleep.

But early the next morning, Tom urged, "Let's go!"

The submarine prospectors submerged and started toward the area of the neo-aurium mine. As they neared the spot, a cry rang out from the sonarman.

"Something's approaching us, skipper! I can't make it out!"

CHAPTER XIX

A TRAPPED SUBMARINE

BRIAN rushed to the scope. A blip of light was moving erratically on the fluorescent screen. Even to the Navy officer's experienced eye, the indications were puzzling.

"On our port bow, Tom, about two hundred feet up!" he reported. "But hanged if I can make it out, either!"

Bud slipped on the hydrophone earset. "Can't hear any engines," he murmured.

"If it's a sub, it may be gliding with its screws stopped," Lieutenant Fraser conjectured.

Tom executed several zigzag maneuvers, then circled the *Sea Hound* back cautiously at a higher depth. Brian continued to watch the scope.

"Still there," he said tensely. "It's slowed down but seems to be following our movements—almost as if it's watching us."

166

"They can't have picked us up on sonar," Bud argued. "Not with our Tomasite coating."

"They could be tracking the sound of our rotor," Brian replied.

Tom decided to risk a direct approach in order to identify the object. At that moment Chow came into the pilot's cabin, an apron stretched taut around his ample girth.

"Brand my oyster stew, what's everyone lookin' so queer about?" he questioned. When Bud told him, the cook gulped. "Oh—oh! Reckon I should 'a' stayed put in the galley!"

Meanwhile, Tom was closing in cautiously on the object as Brian sang out ranges and bearings. Tension heightened almost to the breaking point.

Was the mystery craft a Brungarian submarine waiting to greet them with a deadly fire of torpedoes?

Suddenly a huge gray form loomed into the yellow glare of the *Sea Hound's* searchlight. Tom let out a startled cry.

"It's a whale!"

The relief was so great that everyone broke into laughter. Chow even felt a stir of professional enthusiasm at the sight of so much fresh meat swimming by within easy range.

"Sure wish we had a harpoon gun handy," the old chef muttered wistfully. "I could whomp us up some nice juicy whale steaks!"

"Not on *my* menu," Bud retorted with a wink at Tom. "I aim to keep my teeth, old-timer!"

Chow stumped off, shaking his head gloomily and grumbling, "Some folks jest ain't got the brains to 'preciate tasty new vittles!"

In a few moments they reached the spot where the SFP had shown a heavy concentration of neoaurium in the sea water.

"Switch on the Damonscope, Bud," Tom ordered. "The metal detector, too—and tune the volume."

At once the detector began clicking busily.

"We must be close," Bud reported. "The needle's high in the light-metal frequency range!"

Tom nosed the seacopter slowly up the slopes of the undersea mountain, sweeping the terrain

A huge whale suddenly loomed up

with his search beam. Then, as the detector's clicking became quieter and the needle fell off, he
gunned the rotor and began to descend.

"Looking for the mine opening?" Brian asked.

Tom nodded. "If it's covered, though, we'll
have to probe for it."

As the *Sea Hound* continued its descent, the
clicking became louder again. Deeper and deeper
they plunged, following the terracelike contours
of the mountain's rock shelves. The pressure
gauge showed that they were now more than two
and a half miles under the ocean.

"What is this?" Brian asked, puzzled. "An undersea trench?"

"I doubt it," Tom replied. "The valley floor
probably just slopes lower here than it does where
we anchored the elevator."

Turning the controls over to Bud, Tom in-
spected the Damonscope. Its film developed automatically as the reel progressed. The splotchy
markings on the negative gave definite indication
of radioactive ore, but apparently they had not yet
passed over an open deposit.

Returning to the quartz window of the cabin,
Tom peered out intently. They were now skirting
the very foot of the mountain.

"Bud, maybe we should—"

Tom's words broke off as the detector suddenly
broke into a raucous, frantic clicking of almost ear-
splitting volume!

"Hey! Tune it down! She's going crazy, Tom!"
Bud cried out.

Tom flicked the control knob, threw an excited
glance at the frequency needle, and slid back into
the pilot's seat. The next moment he let out an
excited yell.

"The mine opening! There it is!"

Everyone crowded to the cabin window. In the
yellow brilliance of their searchlight, a large cavelike opening could be seen in the mountainside.
It was clotted with ocean silt. But Tom's pulse
hammered as he realized the opening was clearly
man-made. He could even make out metal sup-
porting pillars inside the mine tunnel.

"You've found it!" Bud slapped the young inventor on the back as the others added their congratulations.

Tom decided to explore the mine opening in a
Fat Man suit. Bud volunteered to accompany him.
As they locked the controls, Brian hastily glanced
at the sonarscope. A second later, his cry sent a
chill of fear through everyone!

"Hang on! Something's coming at us on the
starboard quarter! Terrific speed! I think it's a—"

Tom dived for the controls. But at that same
instant the seacopter shuddered as something
thudded across her top deck. *Bo-o-o-oom!*

The occupants of the cabin were thrown against
the bulkhead as the *Sea Hound* rocked under the
force of the explosion. A torpedo had buried it-

self in the mountainside, sending up showers of
ooze and gravel in the light of their search beam!

Tom flung himself into the pilot's seat and
hauled back on the control wheel. He expected
the seacopter to zoom upward. The submarine
pulled and strained, but remained stationary.

To Tom's dismay, the Sea Hound *was apparently unable to move!*

Tom cut the rotors almost to a dead stop. Under
normal circumstances, the seacopter would have
shot to the surface like a cork. Instead, the only
response was a strange metallic creaking on the
outside of the hull.

"Good grief! What's happened?" Bud gasped.

"Don't know, but we'd better find out fast!"
Tom retorted.

The crew stood by with pale, anxious faces as
the two boys donned Fat Man suits and went to
investigate. The reason for the *Sea Hound's* plight
became apparent instantly.

Cables attached to the buried missile were holding the seacopter firmly to the ocean bottom! A
magnetlike disk on the outer end of each cable
had clamped itself to the *Sea Hound's* unprotected
upper deck. The missile, which had bored deeply
into the mountainside, was thus acting as an immovable anchor.

Bud's face blanched with fear behind his quartz
view plate. "We're sitting ducks, pal! Our enemy
can blow us to bits at will!"

Tom remained calm. "I'm sure they want to capture the *Sea Hound* undamaged," he told Bud. "Our job is to get out of here pronto! We're in no position to fight back, with no missiles of our own! Come inside and I'll tell you a plan I've thought of to free ourselves."

Rushing back aboard, the boys soon emerged again carrying undersea torches to cut through the cables. But as Bud adjusted his torch nozzle and aimed it at one of the steel cables, a fearful cry from Tom came over Bud's sonarphone.

"Stop! Don't cut *any* cable—we'll blow up!"

"Why?" Bud stared at his friend.

"Because they're all booby-trapped!" Tom pointed beyond the *Sea Hound's* deck where the still-settling debris from the explosion partly obscured their vision. "See those cans on the cables out there? Each one has two wires attached. I'll bet my right arm they're bombs!"

"*Bombs?*" Bud gulped.

"If we cut a cable," Tom went on, "those two wires will complete a circuit. Then *whamo!*"

"What can we do?" Bud asked in a low, tight voice.

Tom thought fast. "Bud, here's an idea!" he replied. "I have a small countermagnetizer gadget in the lab that I've been working on. It may not be strong enough to deactivate these magnetic grapples, but we can sure try!"

Hurrying back through the air lock, Tom gave

orders for the countermagnetizer to be brought from the laboratory compartment. Chow ran on the double to get it. Meanwhile, Tom issued other orders to his crew chief and Brian Fraser.

"There's a small portable repelatron in the cargo locker. Set it up in the air lock and tune it for antimissile repulsion!"

Crawling back into his suit, Tom took the countermagnetizer from Chow and clambered out on deck again. He was met by a warning cry from Bud.

"Look out, Tom!"

The next instant, a missile whizzed overhead and exploded against the mountainside! Clutching the guard rail, Tom saw flashes of light in the distance. The enemy was firing a barrage!

CHAPTER XX

A FATHOMS-DEEP SECRET

TOM and Bud in their steel Fat Men could only wait desperately on deck as missiles streaked through the water all around them. Tom counted half a dozen explosions before the barrage ceased.

"Smokin' rockets!" Bud gasped in a trembling voice.

The *Sea Hound* had escaped a direct hit! Inwardly Tom wondered if this was further proof that their enemy wished to capture the seacopter intact. If so, perhaps the missiles had been fired merely to frighten him into surrender.

But there was no time for conjecture and no point in taking chances, Tom told himself. Handing the countermagnetizer to Bud, he reopened the *Sea Hound's* hatch.

"You fellows okay out there?" Brian's voice came anxiously over the sonarphone.

"Roger! And thanks for the fast work on the repelatron!" Tom replied.

The device was set up and waiting in the air lock. Tom lugged it out hastily with his Fat Man arms. He had scarcely positioned it on the deck when another flash of light flared in the distance, then another!

"They're attacking again!" Bud warned.

Tom waited confidently as the first missile came into view. Twenty yards from the *Sea Hound,* it suddenly veered off and ricocheted along the mountainside. Other missiles followed, only to bounce harmlessly off the ship's invisible field, repelled by the force waves from the repelatron!

Tom grinned but said nothing. As the firing ceased, he grabbed up his countermagnetizer, flicked on power, and aimed the focusing tubes at the nearest cable clamp.

There was a sizzling hum of current, then a blue-white flash as the electromagnetic grapple shorted out. The cable dropped harmlessly away from the *Sea Hound's* deck.

"It worked!" Bud cried jubilantly.

Tom aimed his device at the next grapple. One by one, he released each of the cables. "Okay, now get me some nylon line!"

When Bud returned with a coil of the slender, steel-strong rope, the two boys lashed the repelatron to the *Sea Hound's* guard rail and deck cleats.

Then they hurried aboard through the air lock and climbed out of their underwater suits.

"We clear out of here pronto!" said Tom.

Sliding into the pilot's seat, he sent the *Sea Hound* zooming upward. As it broke surface, he reversed the blade pitch and gunned the rotor. The seacopter soared like a flying fish.

Once they were air-borne, Tom radioed an urgent call to the Flying Lab to come at once. Within minutes, the two craft were hovering side by side. A boarding platform was run out and Tom quickly transferred to the *Sky Queen*.

"Did you find the neo-aurium mine?" Mr. Swift asked excitedly.

"We sure did," Tom replied with a wry grin. "But listen to this!" Quickly he poured out the story of the *Sea Hound's* adventure.

"Thank heavens you were able to escape!" Mr. Swift murmured. "Tom, that devilish scheme must have been Decko's work! The warning Ames gave us was—"

He broke off as the radioman's voice came over the intercom. "I've just picked up a call from a Navy sub, the U.S.S. *Marlin*. She's on her way to meet us, radio bearing 085 degrees."

Tom switched on the pilot's radio. "Tom Swift calling U.S.S. *Marlin!* Come in, please!"

The *Marlin's* operator reported that the Navy patrol ships guarding Aurum City had just captured an enemy submarine. When challenged, it had tried to flee, but the United States craft had outraced it and forced the pilot to surrender with two warning torpedo shots. The submarine had then been ordered to surface and had been taken in tow.

"You should sight us any time now," the operator concluded.

Mr. Swift picked up binoculars and scanned the ocean to the eastward. "Here they come!" he said, passing the binoculars to Tom. The *Marlin* was towing the captured craft, with two other Navy submarines accompanying the pair as escorts.

Tom and his father then boarded the *Sea Hound* and swooped down to the water to meet the Navy ships. On invitation from the *Marlin's* captain, Commander Vane, they went aboard.

"Decko!" Tom gasped as he saw the prisoners from the captured submarine lined up below decks. He recognized their heavy-set leader from Longneck Ebber's description.

"You know the prisoner, I see," Commander Vane remarked.

"Only by description," Tom replied. "In case Decko hasn't told you, he tried to destroy my ship, the *Sea Hound,* down on the ocean bottom."

"You can't prove it was us!" Decko snarled.

"He won't have to!" Commander Vane snapped. "You're already liable to prosecution under maritime law for operating an unlicensed vessel of no national registry, and what's more, an *armed* vessel with missile tubes that showed signs of recent firing. My guess is that'll be enough to convict you of attempted piracy."

"And," Mr. Swift put in quietly, "I'm sure the FBI can convict him and his whole gang on charges of espionage."

The words of Commander Vane and Mr. Swift threw the prisoners into obvious dismay. Several were Brungarian scientists, but the others were seamen of assorted nationalities with no strong allegiance to Decko.

"Wait a minute!" one shouted. "If I talk, will you give me a break at the trial?"

Decko tried to threaten him, but was quickly silenced by a Navy bosun. Commander Vane offered no deal, but promised the man that his cooperation would no doubt be taken into account by the judge and prosecution. Tom recognized him as one of Longneck Ebber's two pals whom he and Bud had followed at the carnival.

"Okay. That's good enough for me." The man, whose name was Quidd, revealed that Decko had hired him at the very outset of the plot. He and Longneck Ebber had been the men whom Tom had seen riding in the new Tioga. But it was Longneck, he insisted, who had knocked Tom out.

Later, Quidd had shipped out in Decko's submarine. They had tried to trail Tom's seacopter and the two cargo jetmarines to the city of gold, and had finally managed to locate the site. Decko and his Brungarian associates had counted on the fake letter planted in the chest by Longneck Ebber to establish a Brungarian claim to the city.

When this scheme was foiled, Decko had vowed revenge on the Swifts. His submarine had tried to trap and destroy the *Sea Hound*. Failing in this, too, he had headed toward the city of gold in hopes of sabotaging the air dome, only to be captured by the United States Navy patrol submarines. The story was promptly backed up by several other members of the gang.

"You fools!" Decko stormed. "Do you not realize you are putting a noose around your own necks?"

"Your neck more likely!" Commander Vane snapped.

"Well, son, this seems to clear up everything," Mr. Swift said, turning to Tom.

"Except for that sunken submarine with the skeletons aboard," Tom said thoughtfully.

A look of regret shadowed Commander Vane's face. "I can answer that, Tom," he said in a somber voice. "We've identified it as a secret United States Navy submarine of experimental design, operating on special detached duty. It was overdue and unheard from, but now we know its fate. One good thing, at least, we can be sure at last that no other nation has a prior claim to the gold city."

"What about the tools we found?" asked Tom.

"They were," Commander Vane answered, "the personal keepsakes of the captain who had used them when he was a seaman many years ago. At that time the Varda steelworks were in a free country and our Navy bought many of their tools."

The Swifts were saddened at learning that American servicemen had perished in the sunken submarine, and both returned to the *Sea Hound* in thoughtful silence.

Presently, however, after father and son had waved farewell to the Navy submarine, Mr. Swift said, "Tom, tell me the details about your discovery of the neo-aurium mine."

The young inventor gave his father a full report.

Mr. Swift, his eyes kindling with enthusiasm, exclaimed, "This is wonderful news! If the ancient mine excavations are still open, it should be easy to set up operations using all of your undersea devices. We may even better the rocket contract deadline!"

"I hope so, Dad. Does that mean you'll be flying back to Shopton at once?"

"The sooner the better, son. And you?"

Tom said he wanted to return to Aurum City for a final check on the cleanup work.

"All right. But speed home as soon as you can. I need you to assist me in planning the undersea mining operations."

After warm handshakes and a round of good-bys to the *Sea Hound's* crew, Mr. Swift boarded the Flying Lab again and took off for home. The radio suddenly crackled with a call from Mel Flagler at Aurum City.

"Hurry back here, skipper!" Mel begged. "We've just made a discovery that'll make your eyes pop!"

The *Sea Hound* promptly submerged and sped toward Aurum. Mel, Zimby, and the others rushed to meet them as Tom berthed the seacopter outside the dome.

"We've set up a new air space with the extra repelatron," Zimby reported. "It joins with this one around the city, so we can walk from one to the other. Come on!"

Work was practically suspended as everyone accompanied Tom and his *Sea Hound* crew into the adjoining air space. This extended past the Aurum City canyon into the valley beyond.

A narrow pass opened off the valley on the right. It formed a sort of fiord, leading down toward what had once been a "seashore" thousands of years ago, before the whole land had sunk under the ocean.

A small golden temple stood on the headland overlooking the "sea." It was now in process of being cleaned.

"I never even noticed this building before,"

Tom remarked. "Fine work, fellows. Is this the surprise you wanted me to see?"

Mel winked at Zimby. "Not by a long shot, skipper. Take a look down there!"

Tom's eyes followed Mel's gesture. The next instant, he and his companions from the *Sea Hound* were gaping in amazement.

Half buried in the ocean slime below the promontory lay a strange craft. It resembled the sky wheel which Tom Swift had built as his first Outpost in Space!

"A spaceship!" Bud gasped.

A babble of excited voices now burst out on all sides, besieging Tom with questions. Had the ship crashed after Aurum City was built—or were its occupants the ones who had first founded the city?

Tom shook his head, trying to control his own excitement. "Right now I can't even guess, fellows. But I certainly intend to find out—after I design the special equipment it will take to discover all the answers!"

More thoughtfully he went on, "An advanced spaceship lying here under the ocean for all these thousands of years! I wonder what it's made of?"

"Like you say, we'll find out someday, boss," Chow spoke up. To himself the faithful Texan predicted that it would not be long before Tom Swift Jr. was off on another adventure! And his prophecy proved correct, for Tom soon was to start work on one of his most challenging projects *with his Cosmic Astronauts*.

"In the meantime," Chow went on, "how about a real celebration with all the trimmin's in honor o' Uncle Sam's city o' gold an' Tom Swift's new super-duper rocket-metal mine!"

The crewmen cheered in approval.

"Okay." Tom grinned. "But don't weight us down with too much grub, Chow, or we'll never make it back to the surface!"